Grace Falls

by

H.P. Munro

Grace Falls is a Red Besom book
www.red-besom-books.com

ISBN13: 978-1495400544
ASIN: B00I5UVVN2

Acknowledgements

The question of what to do while on a snowboarding holiday when you're too scared of breaking your backside again while attempting to hurtle down a hillside strapped to a bit of fiberglass, became an easy one to answer. You create a town where you'd like to live – that said you're not sure you would *want* to live there for fear of suffocation or succumbing to the desire to suffocate someone else. Regardless, tucking myself away in Grace Falls, while sampling the après ski (sans actual skiing), was a lovely way to spend time. Therefore, in a roundabout way, I would like to thank the instructor who had so much more faith in my ability to navigate an icy slope than I did, not one to hold a grudge...I was right, I could not do it!

Again, thanks go to anyone who read and remembers this story in its original guise and thanks to my usual suspects of guinea pigs, Angela, Karin, Lesley, and Pauline.

Biggest thanks again go to my wife, for her never-ending support and patience and ability to spot a stray apostrophe at a hundred paces.

For Jane

Contents

Prologue

Maddie Marinelli checked her watch for the fifth time since sitting down, she looked over to the empty seat opposite and sighed. It wasn't the first time that Joanna was late for dinner. In fact, it was becoming a common occurrence. However, this was their anniversary dinner, and Joanna was over an hour late. It had been twelve years since they'd met at Harvard, seven years since they stood in front of family and friends and vowed to spend their life together, and six months since Maddie had noticed small fissures begin to appear in their once strong relationship. However hard she tried to suture the cracks, they kept reappearing.

"Sorry, I'm late. Last minute fuck up with a client."

In one fluid movement, Joanna slid into the seat opposite her wife and waved the waiter over.

"It's okay, I was late too. There was a fire in an apartment building, so the ER was manic," Maddie lied, frowning at her inability to show her disappointment at her wife's tardiness and almost indifferent apology.

"Oh, that's okay then. Have you ordered?"

"Not yet, I was waiting on you."

"Well, I'm here now, and I'm starving." Joanna buried her nose in the menu, using it as an excuse to avoid speaking to her wife.

Their dinner was an awkward affair. The easy conversation that used to flow between them had become a stilted exchange of information and chat usually reserved for polite conversation with strangers. Joanna was on edge throughout the meal, continually running her hands through her short blonde hair and shifting in her seat constantly as if she would rather be anywhere else than in one of Atlanta's top restaurants with her wife. Her one word or apathetic responses repeatedly thwarted Maddie's attempts to keep the conversation going.

When the waiter asked whether they wanted the dessert menu or coffees, Joanna interrupted any response from Maddie to ask for the check. She practically grabbed it from the waiter's grasp when he returned with it.

Maddie was perturbed at their sudden exit. As they stepped out into the warm Atlanta evening, she was still pulling on her light jacket as Joanna stood tapping her foot against the warm pavement. She opened her mouth to apologize in case her choice of restaurant had been the wrong one, but before she could say a thing, Joanna handed her a set of house keys.

"Why are you giving me your house keys?" she asked.

"Because I won't need them."

"What are you talking about? Of course you'll need them." Maddie held the keys out to return them.

"No, no, I won't, Maddie. I'm not coming home with you tonight or any night."

"You're not making any sense, just take the damn keys." Maddie thrust them towards her wife. When she didn't get a response, she grabbed Joanna's hand and tried to put them into her closed fist. "Joanna, please you're scaring me, take the keys."

"Maddie, please don't make a scene."

"What the hell are you talking about, making a scene?" Maddie asked raising her voice. "I don't understand what's happening here."

Joanna cast a quick look around the sidewalk and flashed an apologetic smile towards a passerby. "Please don't shout. I've ordered two cabs for us. One will take you home, and the other is taking me to a hotel, I've cleared my stuff out of the apartment." She took a deep breath. "I'm leaving. I've been offered a job in the New York office, and I've accepted it."

"I'm sorry?" Maddie closed her eyes as if hoping that squeezing them shut would somehow give her insight into why her wife was behaving this way or, when she opened them, she would realize that this had been some form of nightmare daydream. However, when she opened them, Joanna was still standing there with an impatient look on her face. "You're what?"

"Maddie, we both know it's not been right between us for a while. I don't know how or when it happened but we've changed. Neither of us are the people we were when we met or when we married." Her blue eyes pleaded with Maddie to understand.

Despite her best efforts, Maddie could feel tears start to fall down her cheeks. "That's the best that you can come up with? We're different now, so it's over. You're honestly going to throw away a twelve-year relationship without even talking any of this over with me. You're just going to go?"

"This way is for the best. Once you've had time to accept it, you'll see I'm right. If I had spoken to you about how I was feeling you would have just tried harder and lost more of yourself in the process."

"How long?" Maddie swiped at the tears betraying her anger. "How long have you felt this way? How long have you been lying to me about our marriage?"

"Months, years. I don't know," Joanna said, throwing her hands up in the air. "You used to have spirit in you Maddie, but now I think the ER gets the best of you and I get what's left. Even tonight when I was late, you were pissed. You had every right to be pissed, and yet you lied. I know when you left the hospital today, I checked. You just seem to put aside everything for an easy life."

"Easy?" Maddie puffed out a noise that was somewhere between a sob and a laugh. "Seriously? You think that working seventy hours a week in the ER and coming home to dirty laundry and your crap strewn around the apartment is easy. I don't not say things for an easy life, Joanna, I just chose not to spend what little time I had with you fighting. It's called making a marriage work." She lifted her hands and combed her fingers through her black hair until they entwined at the back of her head. "I can't believe that you're trying to put this on me. You're the one telling me, on our anniversary dinner I might add, that you're leaving me to move to New York, and you have the audacity to blame me for the failures in our marriage?"

Joanna gave a half shrug. "It just seemed like you stopped caring."

Maddie threw her a disgusted look. "Take a good look, Joanna, 'cause this moment here. This moment is when I stopped caring." She tugged at the simple gold band on her finger, grimacing as the skin pulled around her knuckle as she removed the ring and threw it towards Joanna's chest.

“And now I’m going to make it really easy for you. The next time I hea from you, it better be about a divorce.”

Chapter One

One Year Later...

Maddie's fingers tightened around the hard molding of the steering wheel of her T-Bird. Her head bobbed around in time to the music keeping her company on her long drive west as the wind coming in from the open windows caused her dark locks to dance to their own rhythm. In four weeks, she would be starting her new life in San Francisco. A new job, a new start. She was almost giddy at the possibilities a clean slate offered her. No-one looking at her with her past failures reflecting in their eyes. No more reminders of could, or should haves. Even the small voice that persistently whispered that she was running away was silent today.

The beginning of a broad smile started to tug at her lips as the song changed on the radio. She reached down and cranked the volume up as far as the dial would allow. Her fingers began to beat the rhythm of the song, and she started to mouth the words silently. As the tempo started to increase, and the chorus began its second repeat, the steady beat she had tapped with fingers became an enthusiastic tattoo as she smacked the steering wheel with the heel of her hand. The silently mouthed words were replaced by a full-throated sing-a-long. Her shoulders danced in time with the music as the upbeat tune reached its crescendo. She felt happy. A word so small that it failed to capture the myriad of emotions careering around Maddie Marinelli at that moment. But if you were to ask her, she would chuckle, shake her head in an almost self-deprecating way and admit, albeit cautiously, that she was indeed happy...and hopeful.

The song changed again to one that Maddie didn't know and, as the signal started to hiss with interference, she rolled her eyes, wondering whether she should bite the bullet and update the radio from the original AM signal seeker radio for a more modern one. Her love for the original features in her car had already stopped her from replacing the Town and Country radio on several occasions. She sighed and twisted the volume dial until it brought the noise down to a more acceptable level before pressing the on/off button and silencing the radio.

In the quiet, she allowed the passing scenery to invade her happy bubble, the brown hue of her sunglasses lending their color to the passing wilderness. A quick glance at her GPRS confirmed her suspicion than she was indeed in the ass-end of Alabama. The road ahead stretched into the horizon, with no turn or bend to deviate it from its approach to the distance. She quickly checked her mirrors. Confident that there were no other vehicles in her eye line, she leaned forward in her seat.

"Let's give you a little blow out, baby," she whispered in an almost seductive tone to her car. She sat back and locked her elbows. Her foot pressed the gas pedal down until the back of it hit the footwell. She whooped as her vintage car took up the challenge her right foot presented it with and it surged forward. The orange speedometer needle danced behind the protective glass, pushing up to numbers that Maddie had never taken it to before. Still cautiously watching in her mirrors in case her antics were being captured by a patrolman, Maddie started to rock back and forth as if egging the car, that was twenty years older than her, on. She was just about to celebrate the fifty-four-year-old engine reaching the top speed that had been on its credentials in its heyday when a loud bang came from the engine, and the car started to slow.

"Nonononononono," Maddie whined as she pressed the brake pedal and pulled the car to the side of the road. She got out and popped the hood open, stepping back to avoid being engulfed in the steam that rose from the engine.

"Not the sort of blow out I had in mind."

Coughing at the acrid smell from the engine, she waved her hands to clear the air. "Well that's not good," she groaned, pushing her sunglasses onto her forehead.

The steam started to clear, and she was finally able to see into the engine, spotting immediately the damage she had caused. She pulled her cell phone from her back pocket and walked around to the driver's door to call Triple A.

"Typical, just typical," she yelled as the screen of her cell informed her that she had no phone signal. She tossed the useless phone through the open window of the driver's door onto the seat where it bounced before landing in the footwell. Maddie gritted her teeth and let out a low growl of frustration, before taking a deep breath and giving herself a mental check. "Okay, this is not a problem. This...this is an opportunity." She faked a smile as she used her hands to shield her eyes from the late afternoon sun, checking out the deserted road in hope. Seeing nothing, she gave her beloved car a kick to the front tire. "And this is where I will die," she growled.

She leaned in through the open window and grabbed her half-full bottle of water, taking a long swig of the lukewarm liquid while formulating her plan. She checked her GPRS again and spotted a town twenty miles ahead. Looking up at the sun she cursed the Marinelli competitive streak that meant she had spent less time and attention to her navigation badge in girl scouts than selling the most cookies. Realizing that any judgment she made on daylight hours left was going to be based more on guesswork than fact, she deduced that the sun would cool off in a couple of hours making the twenty mile walk a bit easier. Her plan, for the time being, was to stay out of the sun and relax. She pulled out a rug from the car, fished out a medical journal from the boxes of her belongings in the trunk, and settled down in the shade of the car to wait it out.

An hour later and nature was calling...loudly. At first, Maddie ignored it, using all of her mind-over-matter techniques that saw her make it through long hours in the ER. However, during work, her laser-like focus on what she was doing could fool her mind. With no such distraction now, her mind had started to question her decision to ignore her body's needs. She managed to last another half hour before her mind had started an all-out rebellion and she could no longer ignore her bladder. Grabbing a handful of tissues, she walked off the road and selected a suitable bush. She quickly scanned the undergrowth for anything that might leap up and bite her ass, before undoing her jeans, pulling them roughly down to her ankles, and crouching. Her eyes rolled back in her head in ecstasy as her bladder started to empty. The sound of her urine hitting the dry sand was, however, suddenly joined by a car engine and loud music.

"Noooooo," Maddie groaned realizing that she might miss her chance of rescue thanks to her bladder. No amount of pelvic floor exercises would have allowed her to stop mid flow.

The engine and music stopped, and Maddie heard the sound of a door opening and closing.

"Hey, is there anyone here?" A male voice yelled from the roadside.

"Yeah, I am, I'm here, gimme a minute," Maddie shouted back urging her body to hurry up. "C'mon," she muttered in encouragement. "Finally!" she snarled as she finished. She pulled her jeans back up mumbling. "Longest pee in history." Hastily refastening her jeans, she half ran back towards her car.

"Oh, hey." A tall man greeted her. He pushed his red baseball cap back on his head, revealing dark blonde hair, and scratched his forehead. "You look like you're in need of some help." He motioned towards the car.

Maddie smiled. "I've cracked the radiator and blown the head gasket."

The man looked at her in surprise. "You a mechanic?"

"No, a doctor. I just like cars, this one especially." Maddie laughed, looking fondly at her car. "At least when it works I do."

"A doctor?" The man seemed to be contemplating something as a look of concentration furrowed his face. Suddenly the look was gone, replaced by a large welcoming smile. "My name's Sam Hunter. I work for an auto shop in Grace Falls. Why don't we get you hitched up and we can have a look at it for you?"

Hesitating, Maddie balanced off her needs for help against her desire not to become a missing person statistic. Her eyes flicked across to the truck Sam was driving. On the side in black lettering was 'Campbell's Auto Shop, Grace Falls' No.1 place for your automobile needs.'

Sam followed her gaze. "It's also the only place in Grace Falls for your needs and the only place for around ninety miles." He laughed. "There's no phone signal at this point on the road, but it comes back in about a mile up if you wanna walk on and phone ahead to check me out." He smiled, sensing the reason for her hesitancy.

Studying his face, Maddie sensed that Sam's offer was genuine. "Okay, let's do this." She smiled, dropping the hood of the car closed.

∞ ∞ ∞

Thirty minutes later after hitching the car to Sam's rescue truck, they were pulling into Campbell's Auto Shop. A dark-haired man with twinkling blue eyes came out to greet them. Smiling broadly, he assessed the classic car on tow. "She's a beauty," he murmured appreciatively while wiping his hands on a rag.

Maddie jumped out of the cab where she had ridden with Sam who had peppered her with questions about her medical career throughout the journey. "Yes, she is. Unfortunately, she's a beauty with a cracked radiator, and blown head gasket."

"Cracked beyond repair," Sam added emphatically.

The dark-haired man winced at his colleague's assessment. "Peter Campbell." He nodded, holding up his oil-stained hands as way of an apology for the lack of handshake. "You might be in luck. I was restoring one of these a few years back. I should still have some parts in store." His smile faltered as he caught sight of Sam shaking his head vigorously behind Maddie's back.

"Maddie Marinelli," Maddie offered, not noticing the questioning look that Peter was throwing towards Sam.

"Doctor Maddie Marinelli," Sam said slowly, nodding his head with wide eyes, waiting for Peter to get onto his wavelength.

Peter's face relaxed as comprehension dawned. "Why don't you have a seat and we'll go take a look in the back." He indicated over to a plastic chair and table. "There's coffee in the pot." He jerked his head at Sam who gave a quick smile to Maddie before shuffling off to catch Peter.

"A doctor?" Peter whispered, keeping one eye on the door to the shop where Maddie sat.

"An ER doc, on her way to San Francisco to start a new job in four weeks. She could be what we need," Sam replied, his excitement raising his voice above a whisper.

"Shhh," Peter admonished. "I have a radiator and gasket that would fit her car." He frowned uneasily at the hint of deception he knew Sam was about to suggest.

Sam gripped Peter's shoulders. "Your wife is about to hatch your first child any day now. Do you want her to have to travel sixty miles to do that, just 'cause we don't have a doctor right now?"

Peter closed his eyes and exhaled softly. "No, but there's no guarantee that she'd go into labor while the doc is here."

"We stall her for two weeks, two and half tops. If Ruth's still got the bun in the oven, we fix the car and let the doc go on her way," Sam reasoned. "No harm, no foul."

Weighing up the options Peter finally turned towards the door. "I'm sorry, Doctor. Marinelli. I don't have the parts after all. I made a quick call, and I can get them shipped here, but it'll be a couple of weeks." He held his hands out apologetically.

Maddie's eyes widened. "A couple of weeks? I'm on my way to San Francisco. I don't have a couple of weeks," she moaned.

Sam stepped forward before Peter changed his mind. "You don't start your job for another four weeks, or so you said earlier," he added hastily seeing Maddie's raised eyebrows. "That's still plenty of time to get there." He smiled. "Peter and his wife have a spare house in town. You can stay there while you're waiting."

The dark-haired man cast Sam a quick glare before clearing his throat. "Yeah, my wife's mama's house is laying empty at the moment, so you'd be doing us a favor. Having someone there I mean," He said absently, playing through in his head how the conversation with Ruth; to explain why a complete stranger was going to be staying in her late mother's home, would play out.

Maddie looked at the two men and sighed. "Two weeks?" she repeated, with a skeptical look on her face.

"Yes ma'am, and a half," Sam inserted. "Tops." He shook his head and waved his hand dismissively.

"Looks like I don't have much choice," Maddie said resignedly. She had hoped on having a bit of downtime in San Francisco before she started work. Now it looked as though her downtime would be spent in Grace Falls.

∞ ∞ ∞

"So our town is going to be one hundred and fifty years old next year," Sam said proudly. "It was named after Ebenezer Grace, and the Grace family still own most of the big businesses that employ the town. They have the lumberyard and hunting lodges, and still own most of the prime real estate too."

"Influential family," Maddie added, looking out of the window.

"Was a time that you couldn't fart without the Grace family having an opinion on it," Sam said gruffly.

Maddie noticed that his face tightened when he spoke about the Grace family. "Not a fan of theirs?" she asked.

Sam shrugged. "Story for another time." He pointed out Ruby's Coffee Shop and Sullivan's Sports Bar as he drove Maddie to the old Anderson house that had belonged to Ruth's mother. Both the bar and coffee shop appeared to be the social hubs of the small town. He also made a point of showing Maddie the town's recently vacated medical clinic, to which she made the appropriate sympathetic murmurs. After helping to carry some of Maddie's boxes into the house, Sam's role appeared to have ended, and he nervously left her alone with a waiting Ruth.

The bemused woman led Maddie into the house where she and her younger sister had grown up. She had been somewhat perturbed by her husband's phone call. It wasn't every day that your husband loaned out your dead mother's house, seemingly at random, to a stranded doctor. Sensibly, Peter had omitted to tell his wife of his part in Maddie's predicament.

"So how much longer have you got to go?" Maddie asked dropping her rucksack onto the hardwood floor of the living room and absently taking in her surroundings. "With the baby I mean," she added.

Ruth smiled. "Anytime now I guess." She cupped her swollen stomach fondly. "The timing is all up to this one now. Emm..."She chewed on her lip. "Well I guess this is the living room, the kitchen is through there." She pointed to a heavy door to the rear of the living room. "There should be plenty hot water, the boiler does it automatically, and I'll be honest I have no idea how to work it. There're three bedrooms and bathroom upstairs, but only the room facing the back has a bed in it now." She gave Maddie an apologetic smile. "Don't worry it's not the one my mama died in." She spun around with her hand over her mouth as she mentally went through everything that she thought Maddie would need, causing her to miss Maddie's wide eyes at her remark about the bed. "I'll pop back with some provisions for you. If you'd like you're welcome to join us for supper?"

Maddie yawned loudly, suddenly feeling the effect of the hours of driving she had done prior to her engine blowing. "Oh my God, I'm so sorry," she effused. "It's been a really long day, I may just shower, and go to bed. Thank you though for your kind offer and for letting me stay here. It's a lovely home." She gave Ruth a grateful smile.

"Well, I hope you get some rest." Ruth smiled and headed towards the front door. "There should be clean bedding and towels in the cupboard at the top of the stairs." She pointed towards the sweeping staircase in the hall. "I'll maybe see you tomorrow. Good night."

Ruth slipped out of the front door and carefully stepped down the stairs towards the pathway leading back towards the white picket fence surrounding her childhood home. Sam was leaning against his pick-up truck, with a smug smile playing on his lips.

"Sam Hunter, you will tell me what is going on with that shit-eating grin of yours before I beat it out of you," Ruth said, heaving herself up into the truck while swatting Sam's helping hand away.

"Whaaat?" Sam said innocently. "I have no idea what you're talking about." He closed the door to the truck and ran around to the driver's door, giving the old Anderson house one last look before jumping into the truck to run Ruth home.

By the time Maddie had made her bed and had a shower, darkness had taken hold of Grace Falls. She padded downstairs to the kitchen still toweling off her dark locks. She smiled as she spotted a box on the counter, surmising that she must have had visitors while she was showering. Tossing the towel onto the chair, she peeked into the contents of the box.

Ruth had packed her coffee, sugar and a note that said that the fridge had milk, eggs, orange juice, and a portion of homemade lasagna in it. There was an addition to the note in a more masculine hand advising that there was also beer in the fridge. Maddie chuckled to herself as she pulled out the coffee and sugar and placed them on the counter. She was amazed at the generosity that she'd experienced so far from the occupants of the town. Opening the fridge, she pulled out the plastic box containing the lasagna and grinned at the cooking instructions taped to the lid. She wondered whether this was one of a set for Peter to tide him over while Ruth was in hospital with the baby.

After a few moments of trial and error, she managed to light the oven and find a bottle opener for her beer. An hour later and she was sated, after polishing off the lasagna, and two bottles of beer. Yawning, she cleaned away her dishes and climbed the staircase towards the back room that was to be her bedroom for the duration of her stay.

As her body relaxed into the soft mattress, the thick blankets and comforters soon had her cocooned in their warmth, and she drifted off to sleep.

She couldn't tell when or what it was that woke her up, but she was suddenly awake and disorientated by the strange surroundings. Glancing at the nightstand, she saw it was one a.m. With a sniff of disgust at being awake, she buried herself further into the bed, determined to recapture her much needed sleep. Uninterrupted sleep was a luxury for an ER doctor, and it had been a while since Maddie had enjoyed the possibility of more than a couple of nights of complete rest. However, five minutes later it appeared that tonight was not going to be one of those nights. A persistent noise invaded her consciousness, and once she was aware of it, she couldn't not hear it. The noise had a rhythm to it. It was as though someone was digging. She found herself counting each thud, waiting on the next one arriving. Unable to return to sleep, she rose and looked out of the window to see if she could spot the origin of the noise. It took a few moments before her eyes adjusted sufficiently to allow her to locate the source of the sound.

Standing in the backyard of the house opposite was a woman. Her blonde hair was tied up in a messy ponytail. As she took a break from digging what appeared to be a rather large hole in the ground, she wiped the back of her hand across her forehead. The movement left a large smear of dirt across her face.

Maddie could not help but continue to watch in curiosity, wondering why the woman would be digging her garden in the middle of the night, and why she would need such a large hole. Her inquisitiveness kept her monitoring the blonde woman's progress until it appeared that the hole had reached its required depth. Maddie craned her neck as the woman dropped her spade to the ground and picked up a package wrapped in a black plastic bag. A soft blue blanket could be seen peeking out one side. She placed the package carefully into the hole then stood up. Resting her hands on her hips, she stretched her lower back out. The change in her position allowed her gaze to drift up towards the deserted Anderson property. A look of shock registered on her face as she spotted a shadowy figure standing in the window observing her before disappearing.

Maddie's mouth had opened in surprise at being spotted, and she'd quickly stepped back into the darkness of the room. She hoped that the woman would think whatever she had seen was a trick of the light.

∞ ∞ ∞

The following morning Maddie awoke to birdsong from the trees outside her window. She rose and looked out of the window to inspect the day, but more importantly to check that what she had seen last night had not been created by her sleep-addled brain. Her memory was soon confirmed. As she stood at the window, she could see clearly the disturbed earth where the woman had been. Maddie frowned as she pulled on her hooded top, zipping it up as her mind still puzzled over the need to bury something in the cloak of darkness.

She entered the kitchen and poured herself a glass of orange juice as her mind drifted towards the nocturnal activity that she had witnessed. Finally, unable to stem her nosiness any further she found herself out in the backyard of her borrowed house. She walked over the harsh blades of grass in her bare feet, the morning dew moistening the bottom of her blue and purple checked pajama bottoms. She edged along the boundary of the garden until she found a gap in the fence that divided the two properties. Pushing through the hedge, she squeezed through into her neighbor's garden and then made her way towards where she had seen the woman.

Now standing over the patch of earth Maddie had no idea what she was going to do.

"Hello. Did you know Buttercup?"

Maddie jumped and spun around startled. She found herself looking into a pair of pale blue eyes, a welcoming smile revealing dimples in either cheek. The young girl tipped her head to the side. Her blue eyes sparkled with curiosity and intelligence beyond her years, which Maddie assessed to be around six or seven.

"I, erm, no," Maddie spluttered, still surprised at being found wandering in her neighbor's garden while in her bed wear. "I never met Buttercup." She finished more confidently, feigning a look of disappointment, which appeared to appease the child.

"She was a good rabbit." The girl nodded solemnly. "But not a dwarf rabbit like my daddy thought he was buying. She was huge!" She opened her eyes to their fullest and held her arms out to illustrate the size of the recently departed rabbit. "I heard my mama say that my daddy was an ass who got robbed when he bought her and that he should have gotten me a dog, 'cause at least we could have walked it," the girl added, stepping forward and fixing Maddie with her gaze. "But she was a good rabbit. I'm Jessica Milne-Sullivan. Who are you?" she asked. Her mouth twisted in consternation as she assessed the adult in front of her.

"I'm Maddie Marinelli." Maddie smiled trying not to frighten the child in the slim hope that she could go back next door without the child's parents knowing that she had been in their garden. "I'm living next door for a while." She pointed back towards the loaned property.

Jessica followed Maddie's gesture, pushing herself onto her tiptoes to see. "You're staying in the old Anderson house," she noted, dropping back down onto the soles of her feet. "Is Maddie short for something? My daddy says that any names that end in 'ie' are usually short for something, and he knows *everything*. He calls me Jess when my mama's not around, but that's a secret 'cause my mama don't like my name getting shortened." Jessica leaned forward nodding earnestly as she shared her secret with Maddie.

"It's short for Madeleine," Maddie replied, wincing as she said her full name, which was usually reserved for family occasions and verbal dressings down from her parents.

"Maddie-Lyn," Jessica said carefully, trying to get her tongue around the name.

"Madeleine." Maddie corrected.

The young girl frowned. "Is what I said," she replied, confused at what the difference was between what she had said and what Maddie had said.

"My daddy owns the bar," Jessica said proudly. "He lets me sit on it and eat nuts. Do you work in a bar?" she asked, plonking herself down onto the moist grass.

Giving a quick look towards the house, Maddie shrugged before dropping down to sit on the ground opposite Jessica, with Buttercup's resting place between them. She plucked a blade of grass and started to play with it absent-mindedly. "I'm a doctor," she replied, writhing slightly against the cool wet of the grass seeping through her thin cotton bottoms.

Jessica, on the other hand, appeared unaffected by any discomfort from her seat. "I'd like to be a doctor when I'm big," she said thoughtfully. "When I was born my daddy said that God wasn't sure that He'd made a mistake by letting me leave Heaven too soon. But the doctors persuaded God that my daddy and mama needed me, so He let me stay. Doctor McNeil said I was two pounds of stubborn."

Maddie exhaled as she processed the information behind the detail that Jessica had just given her. She did not doubt for a minute that Doctor McNeil was right in his assessment. Seeing this seemingly healthy and intelligent child, she would not have thought that she had been a preemie, with all the health complications that could have brought. She did not envy Jessica's parents the struggle they must have had during her early months.

"I'm sure you'll make a great doctor, Jessica." Maddie smiled. "Doctor Milne-Sullivan sounds kinda nice, don't you think?"

Jessica scrunched her nose up. "I have the longest name in my class. It takes me twice as long as everybody else to write it," she grumbled. "An' it's all 'cause my mama and daddy ain't." She screwed her face up and hastily corrected herself. "Aren't married."

Maddie opened and closed her mouth, unsure how to respond to the small child casually running through her family history so nonchalantly while sitting on wet grass. Her young face was so full of innocence at the information she was disclosing.

"Which is 'cause my daddy's a manhole."

"Manhole?" Maddie repeated unsure if she had heard correctly.

"That's what Aunt Teddy calls him when she thinks I'm not listening."

Maddie bit down on her top lip to stop the laughter that was threatening to bubble out as she worked out exactly what Aunt Teddy thought of Jessica's father.

The young girl brought her shoulders up to her ears in a deep shrug. "I think it's something to do with him liking ladies, a lot. But then so does my...Mama!" The girl's attention suddenly switched from Maddie to the blonde woman that Maddie had observed during the night. The woman approached with a look of apprehension on her face as her watchful gaze switched between her daughter and the strange dark-haired woman sitting cross-legged and bare-footed in her garden.

"Jessica," the woman said carefully. "Could you come over here please?"

The girl stood up and dutifully returned to her mother.

"What have I told you about talking to strangers?" She admonished her daughter when she was safely by her side. A look of relief flashed across her features as she firmly gripped her daughter's hand.

"That's not a stranger. This is my new friend Maddie-Lyn. She's a doctor staying in the Anderson house," Jessica said, pointing towards Maddie while looking up at her mother in confusion as to why she was in trouble.

Maddie stood. "Hi, I'm sorry I didn't mean to intrude," she said quickly, conveniently ignoring the fact that intruding was exactly what she'd meant to do when she sneaked into her neighbor's garden. "I had car trouble, and Sam found me. My car is at Campbell's, and it's going to take a couple of weeks to fix." She twisted her upper body towards the Anderson property. "So Peter and Ruth are letting me stay here. I'm Madeleine, well, Maddie really," she corrected, hoping that her full name would be ignored. "Marinelli." She held her hand out giving the blonde woman her best smile in the hope that she would forget about the whole trespassing thing.

The blonde woman still looked slightly hesitant, before stepping forward and offering her own hand in return. A wary smile broke out on her face, showing exactly where Jessica had inherited her dimples. "Alex Milne. Welcome to Grace Falls." She shook Maddie's hand then turned her attention to her daughter. "Honey, you've got to go get ready, or we'll be late."

Jessica hopped on the spot then set off up the garden.

"Yes, ma'am. Bye, Maddie-Lyn," she yelled as she sprinted towards the whiteboard house.

"Bye, Jessica," Maddie shouted in return. She smiled at Alex. "I should..." She pointed back towards the Anderson house. "It was nice to meet you, Alex."

"Nice to meet you too," Alex replied with a hint of wariness still in her tone as she wondered why her temporary neighbor was in her garden in her pajamas talking to her daughter.

Maddie set off, walking awkwardly, thanks to the large damp patch on her backside from the grass. She walked in the direction she'd come from hoping she'd be able to find the gap in the fence again.

"Madeleine," Alex shouted after the departing woman. "There's a gate a little down on the right."

Maddie nodded her thanks, managing not to frown at the use of her full name, and switched her direction towards where Alex had pointed.

It was only then that Alex remembered the figure at the window during the night. She frowned and, as she turned, her eyes stopped on Buttercup's grave. She shook her head as she realized that Maddie must have wondered what she was burying and a small smile appeared on her face, growing into a belly laugh, as she walked back towards her home.

"Alex Milne bunny burrier." She giggled to herself, before entering the house and shouting for Jessica to hurry up.

∞ ∞ ∞

Without a plan, agenda, or her beloved car, Maddie was slightly bereft. She realized that it had been years since she had not had anything pressing on her time. It was a disconcerting feeling for someone used to schedules and activity. After eeking breakfast out for as long as she feasibly could, Maddie entered the living room fighting her impulse to be doing something.

She sucked air through her teeth as she examined the array of books on the shelf, her fingers dancing along the spines. Selecting a copy of 'To Kill a Mockingbird' she sat down and opened the book, which she had not read since school, only to rise ten minutes later sighing as she put the book back in its place on the shelf. Picking up her cell phone she scrolled through her contacts until she reached the name she wanted. Hitting the call button, she lazily dragged her fingers along the bookshelf as she waited for the call to be answered. She smiled as a familiar voice came on the line.

"Hello, Doctor Marinelli."

"Zoe, how's things?" Maddie asked flopping down onto the sofa.

"All's good here. I'm getting all set for your arrival. Your boxes have arrived; I've dumped them in your room. I am so excited. I can't believe that I'm getting my best friend back," Zoe replied.

"Yeah, well about that, you may have to wait a little bit. I know you were planning to take some time off so we could hang out and I could do some sightseeing before starting at the hospital, but I've got a bit of car trouble."

Maddie could hear the exasperated sigh from her friend. She knew she was about to be lambasted again about her choice of vehicle.

"I told you not to attempt the journey in that deathtrap you call a car."

"Hey, you were happy to have me come pick you up at all hours in that death trap during residency I seem to remember."

"Yes, but that was fifteen minutes tops. Not a trek across the country. So what's wrong anyway?"

"It's sort of like a mitral valve going on a heart. It's fixable, but it's going to take them a couple of weeks to get the parts." Maddie winced as she waited for the inevitable response.

"Two weeks!" Zoe shouted. "That means you'll barely have any time when you get here. I had plans for us to go to up into the wine country, and everything, and I really wanted you to get to know Mitchell before you started working together."

"I know," Maddie soothed. "I'm pissed too, but there's not much I can do. Besides you talk about Mitchell so much that I feel like I know far too much about him." Maddie was fairly certain that Mitchell would prefer that a co-worker not know quite so much about aspects of his life. However, as best friend to his girlfriend, Maddie had been privy to some intimate aspects of their relationship thanks to Zoe's apparent lack of filter.

She could almost imagine the pout on Zoe's lips as she came to terms with the news.

"Two weeks to get the parts? It's twenty-twelve! What are they doing, making them from scratch?"

Maddie laughed quietly. "It's a classic car. The parts are specialized you can't just magic them up. Quality takes time Zoe."

"Pfft. You say classic. I hear deathtrap. So where are you anyway?"

"I'm not exactly sure, to be honest. I came off the interstate as it was dull driving and that's when I ran into trouble. I'm in a small town called Grace Falls. Everyone seems nice so far."

"I hope at least it's a decent hotel or guesthouse you're in."

"I'm not in a hotel or guesthouse. The mechanic's letting me stay in his wife's late mother's house."

"Let me get this straight. You, Maddie Marinelli, who can't cope without a Starbucks on every corner, is in Hicksville staying in a creepy old house."

When she was able to get a word beyond Zoe's laughing, Maddie attempted to defend herself, and oddly, she felt the need to defend Grace Falls as well. After she ended the call, she felt buoyed by her conversation with Zoe. However, after only a few minutes the feeling of disquiet returned. She restlessly paced the room before deciding to take a run. It would get her out of the house, use up some of her pent-up energy, and let her see more of her hometown for the next two weeks.

She stood out on the porch in her seldom-used running gear, perched her foot on the small stone stump around the wooden supports of the porch, and stretched out her calf muscle. She performed a few lunges and stretches before shaking her head and muttering, "Who are you trying to kid, Maddie? Just run." She hopped down the stairs and set off at a steady jog to explore Grace Falls.

After twenty minutes of running, Maddie realized that Sam's drive the night before had indeed hit the town's high spots. As she jogged through the streets she collected 'good mornings' from the inhabitants she came across and smiled at the friendly feel of the town. Growing up in Brooklyn, she was not used to exchanging pleasantries with strangers. Her usual approach was to avoid eye contact and try to exude a 'don't mess with me' attitude. Today she felt enlivened by the nods and waves she received as she ran. She stopped on the sidewalk outside the closed Sullivan's Sports Bar. Jessica's father's bar she reminded herself, recalling her conversation with the girl earlier in the day. She laughed as she read the menu stuck to the door, which had the name of the bar altered to 'Sullivan's Sports Bra.'

"You're working up quite a sweat there."

Maddie turned towards the source of the voice. Standing behind her was a tall man. His hair and stubble goatee were peppered with grey, lending him a distinguished quality, which belied his mischievous blue eyes and flirtatious tone. She caught him giving her a subtle eye sweep, assessing her curves.

"You must be the Sullivan of Sullivan's bar," Maddie said, deciding that the 'manhole' or as she suspected 'manwhore' description may hold some water.

The man looked momentarily stunned before hiding it behind a charming smile. "You're not about to serve me a summons or something are you?" His eyes narrowed. "Have we met before?" he asked cautiously, fairly sure that he would have remembered their meeting previously.

Maddie enjoyed the fact that her correctly identifying him had put the cocky man off guard by even a small amount. "Nope, but I have met a big fan of yours," she replied in a teasing tone.

Sullivan's eyebrows furrowed. His nickname from Teddy wasn't without warrant. He was naturally apprehensive when he met someone he didn't know but who knew him. In his experience, however, it was usually aggrieved boyfriends, or husbands, that sought him out, and he had learned to either lie about his identity or duck quickly.

"You did?" he asked carefully. "Who might that be?"

"Blonde, blue eyes, dimples, really cute." Maddie grinned taking pleasure from playing with the man, whose face was showing more confusion as the conversation progressed.

"Alex?" he asked warily.

"Jessica." Maddie chuckled shaking her head. Her expression softened as she realized that her description could also have fitted Jessica's mother just as well.

The bar owner exhaled a relieved breath. "My one and only favorite girl." He smiled proudly at the mere mention of his daughter. "Wait, that must make you the bare-foot doctor."

Laughing at the description, Maddie held out her hand. "The one and only. Maddie Marinelli."

"Matt Sullivan, although everyone calls me Sully," he responded shaking her hand. "Alex said you were hot. She undercooked it. So you're the one that thinks Alex is a serial killer or something?" he said grinning.

"What? No!" Maddie spluttered, blushing in a mix of pleasure at Sully's comment about Alex's description of her and embarrassment over the morning's events. She realized that Alex must have put two and two together and worked out why Maddie was in her garden. "I just was curious, I...I..." She flapped her hands around trying to find the right words to describe what she'd thought. Eventually, she gave up and ran a hand through her damp fringe. "Okay so I thought she was a serial killer or something," she finally admitted.

Sully laughed loudly as he dug his hands into his jeans' pockets, rocked back on his heels and hooted.

"She was burying Buttercup; the biggest rabbit in the history of the world. I swear we had a Great Dane when I was a kid that was smaller than that damn rabbit. I think it had a gland problem or something!" He smiled. "She just didn't want Jessica to see it dead."

"I know that now," Maddie said sheepishly.

"Besides she buries the bodies on the other side of the house since it's not as overlooked." Sully laughed at his own joke. "So you're here for a couple of weeks?" he asked pulling the keys to the bar from his pocket.

Maddie scanned the street, frowning as various eyes in the nearby businesses watched her conversation with the bar owner with interest. "Just until my car gets fixed," she replied returning her attention to Sully. "Then I'm on my way."

Sully twisted the key in the lock. "Well, I hope you'll come pay us a visit at the bar sometime."

Maddie couldn't work out if it was deliberate or if everything that he said just naturally sounded like a proposition. She turned and started to jog off, twisting her head she threw him a flirtatious, 'Maybe,' in response, before picking up her pace and running back towards the Anderson house.

∞ ∞ ∞

"I give him two days," Lou observed from the window of Ruby's Coffee Shop. "Two days and that doc will be another notch on his bedpost." She turned and looked at her boss who was concentrating on the books of the shop. "Does he even have a bedpost?" Lou asked, flopping down into the chair opposite Alex, who was chewing thoughtfully on her pen.

"Mmm," Alex replied inattentively. She looked up and seeing Lou's expectant face, realized she had been asked something. Replaying Lou's words in her head and this time concentrating on them, she frowned in response. "Why are you asking me?"

Lou shrugged as she absently collected crumbs from the table using the pad of her fingertip. "'cause you've got a kid together." She looked up at Alex's wide-eyed stare before dropping her eyes to the table. "I just meant that you know him pretty well, but okay you don't know!" she muttered.

Alex put her pen down and leaned back in her chair. "I don't keep track of Matt's sex life. Basically, because that would be a full-time job in itself and I have my hands full being a mama and running a business, and you should pay less attention to Matt's sex life as well." She knew her assistant harbored a crush on Sully, who to his credit had always been charming with Lou and never taken advantage. This, to Alex, spoke volumes about the depth of his feelings towards the woman. He was too much of a manboy to make a relationship work. So, instead, he slept around with women. The ones he wanted to keep in his life, he didn't sleep with. Alternatively, he could also just be terrified that Peter would pound on him for sleeping with Ruth's younger sister.

"If the doctor sleeps with him, then more fool her," Alex said softly.

"Is she pretty? She looked pretty," Lou said, standing up and collecting a cloth to wipe up the pile of crumbs she'd gathered.

Letting her mind drift back to the morning Alex smiled at the image of the flustered woman, standing barefoot in her hoodie and PJs. Her smile when she introduced herself was dazzling. Her eyes were the darkest shade of brown; like luxurious chocolate. Recalling them now Alex thought it would be possible to lose days looking into them.

"Alex!" Lou waved the cloth in front of her boss's face. "I asked...is she pretty?"

Alex shook her head, to clear the image. She thought of her earlier description to Sully. "Yeah, I guess," she said trying to keep her tone non-committal. She cleared her throat and picked up her pen. Lou seemed satisfied with the answer and disappeared into the kitchen, leaving Alex twiddling her pen, allowing herself another indulgent moment of recalling those brown eyes.

She shook herself out of her reverie, this time requiring more than just a head shake to clear her mind of the image. Reluctantly she turned her attention to the figures in front of her. "God I hope she doesn't sleep with him," she muttered under her breath before focusing fully on balancing her accounts.

∞ ∞ ∞

Maddie climbed the steps leading up to the Anderson house, frowning as she spotted a figure sitting on the swing of the porch. "Can I help you?" she asked.

The tall man stood up, running his large hand over his bald head.

"Doctor Marinelli, I presume?" he greeted her smiling.

Maddie returned his smile. "Word really goes fast in this town," she remarked.

"You have no idea." He chuckled. "Timothy McNeil."

Shooting him an apologetic look for her clammy hand, Maddie's eyes narrowed in recognition. "Doctor Timothy McNeil?" she asked.

"Word really does go fast in Grace Falls," he replied. "There are no secrets in this town."

Maddie laughed. "I was talking to one of your success stories this morning, Jessica Milne-Sullivan. Would you like to come in for a drink?" She opened the front door to the house and invited the older man inside.

"Ah, young Jessica." He grinned as he followed Maddie through the living room towards the kitchen. "A precocious young thing. Although that's not altogether surprising with her parents." He sat down in the seat indicated to by Maddie and watched as the young doctor busied herself making their drinks. "She was a fighter. Two pounds of stubborn. She got that from her mama."

"And her charm from her dad." Maddie smiled, filling the kettle with water. "I met him earlier."

"Oh, I'm not so sure about that. Alex Milne can charm the birds from the trees when she wants to," McNeil replied fondly. His tone then switched to a businesslike manner. "Doctor Marinelli, I won't beat around the bush. I believe you're going to be here for a few weeks."

"Two." Maddie corrected. "And a half tops," she added, using Sam's prediction.

He nodded as if contemplating her words. "I wondered whether you might consider providing the town with your expertise during your stay?" McNeil asked. His were fingers pressed together so that it almost looked as though he was praying.

Maddie cocked her head processing his request. "In what capacity exactly?" she asked.

"Doctor Marinelli, I retired six months ago to look after my wife after her stroke, and since then we've had seven locums. They never last more than a few weeks. One lasted a day. The last one left four weeks ago, and we've been without a doctor in the town since. Our medical clinic closed and our equipment got shipped sixty miles away to St Anton's medical facility, along with our nurse."

Maddie was surprised that people had struggled to settle in the town. Her experience, ignoring the inadvertently accusing her neighbor of being a serial killer, hadn't made her think that it would be a hard place to make a life. Perhaps the small town attitude and interest in each other's business could be a bit cloying, but to have gone through so many doctors in such a short space of time struck Maddie as unusual.

"Why so many?" she enquired as she poured water into the coffee mugs. "Doctors, I mean. That's a lot of doctors to go through."

Timothy rubbed his thumb against the table. "This is a tough town. We buried a man last year, seventy-four years old, he moved here when he was eighteen, and he was still known as Old Bill from St Anton. They can be a hard nut to crack." He smiled affectionately as he thought about the town where he had been born and raised. "None of those doctors were accepted by the town. In Grace Falls, it's a case of treating the people, not just their illnesses, and I'm not sure those doctors got that. So regardless of whether they wanted to stay or not, the town canceled their contracts." He sighed. "The phrase 'cut off your nose to spite your face' was created for Grace Falls." He gave Maddie a smile of thanks as she placed a cup of steaming coffee in front of him.

Slipping into the seat opposite, Maddie sipped her coffee carefully. "I don't see what difference it would make. I mean I'm an Emergency Room doctor. I haven't practiced family medicine. Plus, I'm not going to be here for long, and then you'll be in the same position once I'm gone." Maddie shrugged, while she was sympathetic to the situation she was also hesitant about giving up her hard-earned vacation time for a situation that would not improve despite her sacrifice.

Timothy placed his barely touched coffee down on the table. "I thought that would be your answer, but I promised I'd ask." He pulled a piece of paper out of his pocket and slid it across the table towards Maddie. "My contact details, in case you change your mind."

Maddie left the piece of paper untouched, worried that handling it would provide the man with the false hope that she would reconsider. "I wish I could help, but I can't see how I could make a difference."

Nodding, the older man picked up his coffee cup and started to question Maddie on her work and advancements that had been made in treatments, taking enjoyment from the opportunity to flex no longer used knowledge.

∞ ∞ ∞

"Maddie!" Ruth shouted poking her head around the front door of her mother's home. "You in?"

"Through here," Maddie yelled in response from the living room where she'd finally settled down to read a medical journal, following her unexpected but ultimately entertaining visit from the town's former doctor.

"Oh hey." Ruth smiled in greeting. "I was wondering if you'd like to come to join us for supper tonight?"

Dropping her journal onto her lap, Maddie sat up straight on the sofa. "That would be lovely. Can I bring something, dessert maybe?"

Ruth shook her head. "Just yourself, 'bout seven? We're six houses down on the right. The one with the blue fence."

Maddie nodded her agreement. "I'll see you then." She rose to see Ruth out as the heavily pregnant woman walked back towards the door.

Maddie stood on the porch watching Ruth waddle down the path, stopping as she reached the bottom to greet a passing Alex and Jessica. Maddie waved a greeting and hesitated going back into the house, choosing instead to watch as Alex tossed her head back laughing at something Ruth said to Jessica, causing dimples to appear deep in her cheeks.

"Birds from the trees," Maddie murmured thoughtfully. "With those dimples, I don't doubt it." She smiled and turned back to the house.

Alex half-listened to Ruth, as she kept the dark-haired woman on the porch in her peripheral vision. She refocused her attention on the conversation as she became aware that the brown eyes that she had been thinking about earlier in the day were no longer trained on her.

∞ ∞ ∞

"Don't you have a load of old T-Bird parts in the garage from when you were fixing your one up a while back?" Ruth asked Peter, as she passed the potatoes towards Maddie.

"I do, just not the parts that Maddie needs," Peter said awkwardly, looking intently at his plate in order to avoid his wife's gaze.

Lou picked up the vegetables and started to spoon some onto her plate. "So you met Sully today?" she asked Maddie casually.

"Jessica's dad? Yeah." Maddie smiled warmly as her mind flitted to the small child.

Seeing the smile, Lou took it as a reference to Sully. "He's got a terrible reputation you know," she spluttered, hoping she could put Maddie off.

"Lou!" Ruth glared at her sister.

Maddie snickered at the comment. "It's okay. She didn't say anything that I haven't heard already, and from speaking to him, it's no doubt deserved."

"Even though." Ruth glowered at her sister. "Sully is our friend."

Peter laughed at the newcomer's assessment of his oldest friend and the chastisement of his sister-in-law, ignoring the look of annoyance that Lou shot him.

Passing the potatoes on, Maddie picked up her cutlery and started to cut up the chicken breast on her plate. "I know I don't know either of them at all, but I just can't see them together."

"Oh, they're not," Lou interjected, leaning forward with her fork poised in midair as she was about to go into Sully and Alex's history, before spotting another warning glance from her sister and sitting back to eat silently.

Ruth gave her a small nod. She was well aware that Maddie would no doubt be given all of the gory details about their friends while she was in Grace Falls, but was determined that it wouldn't be over her dinner table. She turned her attention to Maddie. "They actually have a lot in common," she said, keeping her tone neutral as she kicked her husband under the table as he added a muttered, 'some fairly specific things,' under his breath.

The conversation moved on, from Sully and Alex to the rest of the town as they regaled Maddie with stories about the colorful personalities, past and present, in Grace Falls.

"Thank you for a lovely meal and a wonderful evening," Maddie said as she hugged Ruth.

Ruth gave the tall doctor a tight squeeze in return, "It was our pleasure. You sure Peter can't drive you home?" she asked half-turning into the house ready to shout her husband.

Maddie smiled gratefully. "It's a lovely night and only six houses. I'm going to walk and enjoy it, thanks again."

She stepped down from the house and started to walk back towards the Anderson house. Her mind started to replay snippets of the evening's conversation as she walked. She had enjoyed listening to the various stories that the three Grace Fall inhabitants had told her. She had found herself paying particularly close attention to the stories that involved Alex. From what she could piece together Peter, Sully, Ruth, and Alex had all known each other since childhood, and had been in the same year at high school.

Despite what Ruth had said about Alex and Sully having a lot in common, Maddie still couldn't picture the two as a couple. She shook her head trying to dislodge the vision of the blonde woman from her mind. "Seriously, Maddie, you do not need to get infatuated with another blonde and blue-eyed woman." She rebuked herself shuddering slightly as she thought about the Joanna debacle; one of her reasons for looking for a fresh start away from Atlanta.

Dressed in her PJs, Maddie hugged a mug of hot milk and examined the contents of the bookcase looking for something that she recalled seeing earlier that day. She grinned as her eyes located the red-bound book, its gold lettering announcing the class year. She pulled the high school yearbook out of its place and took it across to the sofa. Curling her legs underneath her, she sat on the comfortable cushion.

Unsurprisingly Sully was the star quarterback of the football team. She was surprised, however, at Peter who was a lot heavier in his teenage years and had been in the orchestra. "He's grown into his looks," she mumbled turning the page of the book while sipping her hot drink. She laughed as she spotted Ruth and Alex in a group shot of the cheerleading squad. "Really! They were cheerleaders?! They're full of surprises," she remarked.

As she turned the pages to the rogues' gallery mugshots that are inevitable in yearbooks, she flicked past the pages until she reached where Alex's photo would be and frowned at the photograph beside Alex's. Familiar blue eyes and dimples looked out at her. However, this set belonged to a more masculine face. Underneath the photo was the name Alan Milne along with a handwritten message to Ruth.

Ruthie,

When you get tired of band boy, you know where I am...only kidding Peter. There's as much chance of this as there is of my sis and Sully getting it on.

Bear

Maddie couldn't remember any mention in the conversation of Alex having a brother, by either his real or apparent nickname. She laughed at an addition to the note. It was in the same meandering handwriting as the message next to Alex's photo.

The world would freeze over, Pooh before that would happen...not if it were only me and him left in the world...although I do love you, Matt.

Alex

The third entry on the note made Maddie laugh louder. It would appear that Sully was the last to sign the book. His photo was situated only a couple down from the Milne siblings.

I'm hurt...you knew I was going to read this right! You could have at least kept up the pretense of friendship until after graduation. Ruthie, if you grow tired of Grease Monkey then choose me over Bear (we all know he's going to marry Teddy anyway...jeez with their names they're made for each other)

And Alex...you know that I'm the ONLY man for you x

Sully

Maddie closed the book wondering what had happened to Alan Milne and what had changed Alex's mind about Sully from being the last man on Earth to having a child with him. She placed the book on the coffee table and went to the kitchen to wash her mug. As she stood at the sink, she looked out of the kitchen window towards Alex's home. A single light was on upstairs in the house. Maddie watched as it disappeared and plunged her neighbor's house into the darkness of the night.

∞ ∞ ∞

Loud banging roused Maddie from her sleep. It took a moment before her brain processed that the banging was at her front door. She checked the clock. Its blinking LED told her that it was two a.m. Immediately she was wide-awake. She grabbed her hoodie zipping it as she ran downstairs. She had barely opened the door when Alex barged past her with a wheezing Jessica clutched to her chest.

"I need your help," Alex gasped.

Maddie closed the door, her demeanor immediately switching into professional mode. "Tell me what happened?"

"She has asthma. She woke up struggling to breathe. I've given her the inhalers, but they're not working. Nothing is helping. Please help." Alex spoke quickly, practically yelling to be heard over the sound of Jessica's desperate gasps. Her eyes begged Maddie as she tried to disguise her growing panic so as not to alarm the already terrified child. "This happened a year ago, and she was okay when they put her on the nebulizer." Alex swept a hand over her daughter's clammy forehead, wiping the soft blonde curls to the side. The small child struggled to catch even the smallest breath. Her eyes looked at her mother and Maddie in fear.

Maddie grabbed her medical bag from the living room where Sam had dumped it when she arrived. She pulled out her stethoscope and quickly listened to Jessica's chest. "Okay. Let's get her to that nebulizer right now," she said calmly giving the young girl an encouraging smile.

"It's not here," Alex sobbed, her own breath starting to heave as the tears she had been holding at bay started to fall. "It's in St Anton with the rest of the equipment from the clinic. It's sixty miles away. Please help her," she said desperately.

Maddie covered her mouth with one hand as the other one pulled her hair back off her face. This was not good. She begged her mind to think. The St Anton clinic was too far away to get Jessica to in her current condition. This was why she had said no to Timothy. She wasn't a family doctor. She was used to hospitals with equipment and supplies and support. She pressed her fingertips to her lips forcing her brain to stay on track and not to panic. She punched the air as she thought of a solution. "Follow me."

She ran up the stairs two at a time and grabbed towels from the cupboard as she went. She entered the bathroom. "Take her top off," she instructed Alex as she turned the hot water faucet in the shower on full. She was careful to avoid contact with the almost instantaneous scalding water. "Sit down." She pointed to the toilet, then closed the door to the bathroom using the towels to block the gap beneath the door. "Jessica, can you play 'Simon says' with me?" she asked still trying to keep her tone calm. "I need you to put your hands on your head like this." She clasped her hands on the top of her head as the steam from the shower started to fill the room. "Maybe Mommy can help." She smiled at Alex, as the girl struggled to hold her hands in position, her chest heaving with the effort of trying to breathe. Alex took her daughter's hands as instructed. "It creates less pressure on the lungs," Maddie said encouragingly to Alex as she took her stethoscope out to listen to Jessica's chest again. "Now we give the steam a few minutes to work its magic." She gave them both a smile while praying that it would work.

Maddie puffed air up towards her fringe lifting the hair for just a moment and giving her some respite from the damp warmth of the steam-filled bathroom. She was grateful that the house seemed to have an endless supply of hot water as it continued to splash against the closed shower cubicle. She wiped a hand across her damp forehead. The heat was starting to get to her. She unzipped her hoodie and slipped it off her shoulders.

It had taken twenty minutes, but Jessica's breathing had eased, and she lay back in her mother's arm, exhausted by the trauma her small body had endured.

Alex watched Maddie remove her hooded top to reveal a white tank top. Beads of sweat glistened against her olive skin. She looked down at Jessica who had drifted off to sleep and placed a delicate kiss on her daughter's damp blonde curls. Leaving her lips pressed against her daughter's head, she squeezed her eyes tightly closed feeling the anxiety of seeing her child struggling to breathe finally start to leave her body. A noise from the doctor made her eyes spring open. Maddie was gathering some of the towels she had brought into the bathroom and was placing them on the floor.

"Do you want to lay her down for a bit?" she said softly.

Alex responded with a tired nod then shifted carefully so as not to wake Jessica. She gently placed her on the makeshift bed Maddie had created, then slumped onto the floor, letting her head thump back against the wall.

Maddie closed her eyes, taking a deep breath while thanking God that the child had recovered from her attack.

"Thank you."

Maddie opened her eyes and gave Alex a kind smile.

"I...I..." Alex started to speak, but the emotion and relief engulfed whatever she was attempting to say. Her face crumpled, and her mouth moved wordlessly as tears started to spill down her face. Her body wracked with silent sobs as she tried not to wake her sleeping daughter.

"Hey," Maddie soothed, scooting over the bathroom floor and taking Alex into her arms. "It's okay, she's okay." Her lips brushed against Alex's curls as she held the woman tight and feeling her slight frame collapse against her.

Letting all of the tension leave her body, Alex closed her eyes and allowed herself a moment in Maddie's arms to be supported, to be held, to be allowed to be weak. Finally, when she felt exhausted from the release of her tension and emotion, she sniffed and opened her eyes. "She's all I have," she murmured against the skin of Maddie's shoulder. "She's all I have left. Thank you." Alex pulled back from Maddie's embrace to look into her eyes. "I can't thank you enough."

Maddie cleared her throat feeling light-headed from a mix of the heat in the small room and how good it felt, despite the situation, to have Alex in her arms and, right now, the intensity of Alex's stare. Maddie felt as though those blue eyes, still misted with tears, were boring holes through her skull, reading every thought.

"I'm just glad I could help. We'll give her another ten minutes in the steam just to be sure," she said, trying to maintain her professionalism. Alex nodded and reached up to pull a strip of toilet paper from the roll to blow her nose. They both settled with their backs against the cool wall watching almost hypnotically the steady rise and fall of Jessica's chest. "Soooo. You were a cheerleader?" Maddie said with a small smirk on her face. The woman sitting next to her looked over in surprise.

"How'd you know that?" Alex laughed, pulling off the cardigan she had thrown on when she had heard Jessica crying for her from her bed. "Jeez, no such thing as privacy in this town."

Turning to face the blonde woman, Maddie gulped at the sight that greeted her. Alex was now sitting wearing a thin purple camisole.

"Emm." She closed her eyes to concentrate on the ability to speak. "I was at Ruth's earlier," she replied quickly, turning her head away to stop her gawping at the woman. "Aaaand I found your yearbook in the living room."

"Oh God," Alex groaned, laughing. "Yes, I was a cheerleader. Don't hate me."

Maddie tilted her head towards Alex. "You looked cute in your uniform." She smiled, receiving a raised eyebrow in return from Alex.

"I think the word you were looking for was *hot.*" Alex laughed nudging Maddie's shoulder with her own, relieved to be laughing after the stress of the night.

"Okay, hot then!" Maddie chuckled. "Have you never thought about leaving here?" she asked, thinking about her own desire to get far away from everything that was familiar and wondering what kept people in places like Grace Falls.

Alex sighed, her eyes still trained on her sleeping daughter. "We traveled around so much with my dad's job when I was a kid that I never really felt like I had roots until we came here." She rested her head back against the wall, looked towards the ceiling and gave a mirthless laugh. "Even when I thought I was desperate to move away and go to college I only got as far as Tuscaloosa. Then" —she sighed at the series of losses that she had endured— "while I was at college my grandma died and then after I graduated my grandpa had a stroke and needed to be cared for. So I looked after him until he died, then my brother was killed serving in Afghanistan."

"Pooh?" Maddie added, not realizing she had said it aloud.

Giggling, Alex looked at Maddie. Her facial expression was now one of mock-serious. "Oh, he definitely preferred Bear from a gorgeous woman. I was the only one to call him Pooh apart from our mama. She was the one to give him the nickname Pooh Bear and me Piglet when we were small. We're twins, and our names are Alan and Alexandra Milne. When someone pointed out that we were A and A Milne to Mama, the Winnie the Pooh stuff started." She gave a small, sad laugh at the memory or her mother. "She died when we were ten, which is how we ended up in Grace Falls. She was from here and 'cause my dad was in the army and always moving around we moved here to live with our grandparents. So, yeah, calling him Pooh was definitely sister's privilege." She coughed, realizing that she had just told Maddie inadvertently that she was gorgeous and shifted awkwardly trying to hide her embarrassment. "I should point out that no-one has called me Piglet since I was eight."

"Hmm, gorgeous huh, I can accept that." Maddie smiled flirtatiously, thrilled at the compliment from Alex, albeit accidental. "I'm sorry for your loss."

They sat silently for a moment before Maddie spoke again. "He seemed really popular from what I saw in the yearbook."

Alex nodded. She was pleased to be talking about her brother. Even after all the time that had passed their friends seemed unable to come to terms with his death and were always careful to avoid mentioning him. "Yeah, he was, particularly with the ladies. He and Matt were terrible together. I think me and Ruth were probably the only two females in the county not to have slept with either one of them."

"Ah, Sully the 'manhole' according to your daughter."

Alex's eyes widened in surprise at Maddie's remark, before settling on her now softly snoring daughter.

"She overheard someone called Teddy apparently," Maddie explained.

Narrowing her eyes, Alex gave a half laugh. "Claudia Roosevelt, I will kick your ass," she muttered. Then, seeing Maddie's bemused expression, she shrugged. "Sorry, that's Teddy's real name. I'll have words with her to make sure she's more careful. So, anyway, after Pooh died, my dad got sick and retired here. I looked after him until the end, and after he died, I stayed. I had no family left but Grace Falls is home, and honestly there's nowhere else I'd rather be."

"And Jessica?" Maddie probed gently.

"You mean you haven't heard the story yet?" Alex asked with surprise. "Maybe there are secrets in this town after all!" She laughed dryly. "Or maybe you've just not spoken to enough people yet. It was a scandal at the time." She shook her head and prepared to tell the story of how her daughter came to be. "When I hit thirty, my biological clock started ticking so loud that I swear it could have been picked up on the Richter Scale." Alex smiled. "So I enlisted Matt's help. He's too much of a manchild to have a relationship work, but he was desperate for kids. His parents were lousy, and I think he wanted to prove to himself that he could be better, so he was happy to lend a hand." She snorted as she realized her pun. "Literally."

Maddie's mouth opened in surprise. "Ah, so you two weren't together...together?" The strong sense of relief she felt at the realization surprised her. "You know I really couldn't picture you two together," she added.

"Oh God please don't." Alex laughed running a hand through her hair. "Let's say I love Matt. He's been one of my best friends from when we first moved here, but he's *reeeeally* not my type." She stressed in reply, glancing sidelong at the doctor sitting next to her. "He's a great father though, and a great guy once you get past the 'manhole' thing." She laughed. "The thing with Matt is the women he really cares about; he doesn't try and sleep with them. Well, now he doesn't. When he was younger anything that had a pulse was fair game." Her mind drifted towards Lou, as she convinced herself that she was trying to dissuade Maddie from Sully for her assistant's sake and not because of any attraction she felt towards the doctor.

Yawning, Maddie moved onto her knees and picked up her stethoscope. "Good to know! What about you?" she asked keeping her tone neutral as she listened to Jessica's chest. The sleeping child swatting a hand at the cool metal on her chest generated a smile from both Maddie and Alex.

"What about me?" Alex asked carefully, deliberately stalling her answer.

"You don't have someone that you care about enough not to sleep with them?" Maddie asked playfully, settling back down beside her.

Alex snorted. "If we go by that yardstick. I care about a whole mess of people!" She sighed. "I've been focused on Jessica and work. It doesn't leave me time for much else, and I'm not sure that someone I like is just gonna fall in my lap."

Maddie gave her a sympathetic smile. "I know what you mean, but" —she got to her feet—"you never know what's around the corner." She completed her examination of Jessica. "Her chest sounds good. I think you two should stay over." She caught a slight flicker in Alex's eye. "To save you taking her out into the cold," she added quickly, frowning as she realized that it was probably a balmy seventy degrees outside, even at the late hour. "Plus I can keep an eye on her. You two can have the bed. I'll sleep on the sofa."

"Thank you," Alex replied gratefully moving to pick up Jessica, who grumbled in her sleep at the movement.

Once satisfied that both were tucked up safe in the double bed, Maddie went down the stairs and sat down on the sofa. The night's activities finally caught up with her, and she slumped back, letting her head fall against the back of the sofa. Her tired brain still wouldn't allow her to switch off from the drama that had appeared at her door. She stood up, zipped up her hoodie, and slipped out of the front door into the night.

Timothy McNeil switched on his bedside light. He checked his wife was still sleeping soundly beside him before grabbing his dressing gown from the bottom of the bed and slipping his feet into his waiting slippers. He was still pulling his robe around him as he padded down the stairs. In all his years as Grace Fall's doctor, he was accustomed to being summoned in the middle of the night by patients. However, this would be the first time it had happened since his retirement. His ex-patients were understanding and respecting the reason for his premature departure from the post. He switched on the porch light and opened the front door.

Maddie spun around from looking out towards the street. "I'm sorry to wake you. I'll do it."

Timothy looked at her quizzically.

"I want the equipment returned to the clinic first thing in the morning, starting with the nebulizer." She gave him a quick smile then hopped down the stairs. "Nice jimjams by the way," she called from the gate.

McNeil watched her departure then shook his head and chuckled. “Looks like we’ve bagged ourselves a doctor.” He turned back into his home and snapped the lights off.

Chapter Two

Maddie woke slowly. The cover that she had pulled around herself during the night slipped as she shifted, starting to stretch her limbs out from their cramped position on the sofa. She winced as she moved her head, feeling her neck complain immediately about the angle that she had slept at. She opened her eyelids gradually allowing the light to enter and jumped as two blue eyes, inches from her own, came into sharp focus.

"Jessica!" she exclaimed pushing herself back into the sofa in surprise.

"We slept here," Jessica said, more as a statement than a question.

"You did." Maddie smiled. "How are you feeling?"

The young girl rubbed her chest, and the heel of her hand moved the small monkey's face on the front of her pajamas. "Sore," she replied.

Maddie sat up looking around for her stethoscope which she'd lain down somewhere in her tiredness during the night. Spotting it across the living room, she padded over to collect it. She listened to Jessica's chest giving a relieved sigh at the clear breath sounds she heard. "You sound much better." She smiled at Jessica. "How about we make some breakfast. Is your mommy still asleep?" Jessica nodded then followed Maddie into the kitchen. "Would you like some orange juice?" Maddie asked. "Then maybe I can make us some eggs or French toast?"

"Orange juice please," Jessica replied, remembering her mother's instructions on manners. "An' then French toast."

"Excellent." Maddie smiled taking the items from the fridge and getting a glass. "Does your mommy like coffee?" she asked as she poured a glass of orange.

Jessica accepted the glass with a look of incredulity. "She owns a coffee shop," she replied slowly in response.

Maddie narrowed her eyes. "That would be a yes then." She turned and started to make a pot of coffee muttering under her breath. "Fifteen-love to the child." She heard movement behind her, glancing up she caught sight of Jessica in the reflection of the window. The young girl was stretching across the table to reach Maddie's iPad. "Would you like to play a game while I'm getting breakfast?"

Blue eyes widened in excitement. "Can I?" She held the iPad out to Maddie, who switched it on.

"Okay, we have Angry Birds?" She looked at Jessica, who shook her head furiously, causing her blonde curls to bounce around. "Nope? Okay, we have Tetris?" again she received a shake of blonde curls in reply.

"Do you have poker?" the girl asked sipping her orange juice.

"Actually I do," Maddie said scrolling through the screens to locate it. "Wait, you're a kid, you're not playing poker," she exclaimed stopping her search for the application.

Jessica shrugged. "My daddy taught me."

Maddie looked at her in surprise, she released her breath in a quick surge of disbelief. "Okay, poker it is." She opened up the application and handed the iPad over with a look of resignation. "I better not get in trouble with your mom for this," she warned the small child, who grinned at her in response before turning her attention back to the iPad and furrowing her forehead in concentration. Maddie shook her head and resumed her coffee making.

Coffee in hand, Maddie climbed the stairs and knocked gently on the bedroom door. Getting no response, she pushed it open. She smiled at the sight of Alex in the middle of the bed, lying on her back still asleep, with one arm thrown carelessly above her head. Maddie walked quietly around the bed and placed the cup of coffee down on the nightstand, as she turned to walk away she heard a murmur coming from the bed. She turned back to see Alex waking, her face wrinkling at the effort.

Maddie couldn't help but stare as Alex, still with her eyes closed, started to twist on the bed arching her back and moaning at the muscle stretch. The action caused the strap on her camisole to slip from her shoulder. Maddie bit her bottom lip and reluctantly decided to let Alex know of her presence. "Morning," she said quietly, her voice laced with burgeoning arousal. She coughed quickly to clear her throat and blushed at the effect that seeing Alex in her bed had created.

Alex's eyes opened slowly. "Mornin'," she replied sleepily as she looked to her side where the sheets still held the imprint of Jessica's body.

"She's downstairs in the kitchen, her chest sounds clear and none the worse for scaring us both to death," Maddie said pre-empting Alex's likely query. "I brought you coffee." She smiled pointing to the nightstand where the coffee cup sat with steam rising gently from it. "I wasn't sure how you took it." She shrugged apologetically.

"I could get used to waking up like this," Alex murmured sitting up and fixing the strap on her camisole as she reached for the cup. She paused as she realized the possible implications of her words. "With coffee I mean. I can't remember the last time someone brought me coffee in bed," she added quickly, her cheeks flushed with embarrassment.

Maddie gave a soft chuckle. "Well, come downstairs when you're ready. There's going to be French toast."

Alex's eyes widened over the top of her coffee cup. "You don't have to really, you've already done so much," she said taking a careful sip.

"I don't mind." Maddie smiled. "Oh do you know that your daughter is a card shark?" she asked fiddling with the comforter at the end of the bed. "She's playing poker on my iPad. I hope that's okay?" she asked as her brow creased with worry.

Alex laughed. "It's okay. Her dad is a bad influence on her in that respect. Is your iPad connected to the internet?" she asked with a hint of concern in her tone.

Maddie shook her head. "No, no signal. Oh, there's nothing on there that isn't kiddie friendly," she added quickly plunging her hands into the pockets of her hoodie.

"Oh, it's not that." Alex smiled. "My daughter has a past record." She rolled her eyes. "Eight months ago she wanted a horse. We said no, so she got my credit card and bought one on eBay!"

Maddie chewed on her lips trying not to laugh.

"It's okay you can laugh," Alex assured her. "We did, once we got the seller to understand what happened. She's smart for her age. We've got her on an accelerated program at school 'cause she's too clever for her own good!" She laughed. "So she has no internet privileges until she's sixteen." They shared a laugh, then Alex started to look around the room. "God, I've not been in this room since I was a teenager." She smiled. "In fact the last time I was in the room I was on this bed." She smiled at the memory her palm touching the mattress as if lifting the memory from it. "And if it hadn't been for Matt I would have lost my virginity here." She laughed as more of the memory returned. "God poor Charlotte Grace. Her face was a picture." She stopped and winced, slowing lifting her eyes to meet Maddie's. "Sorry, oversharing. So, French toast!" she said brightly as she smiled broadly at Maddie who was smirking at her.

"Ruth told me it was a different bed and not the one her mom died in."

Looking at the bed, Alex's brow furrowed. "Looks the same," she commented dispassionately. Her face screwing up as her brain processed the implication. "Eww, God, I so hope it's not." Her mouth twisted in disgust.

"Let's just believe that it's new," Maddie said standing up. She walked to the door. "French toast in ten and Alex, you do remember that this town apparently has no secrets. So if I want to find out about you and that bed, or should I say its predecessor, I probably could." She grinned and left Alex sitting on the bed shaking her head.

"I have no doubt about that, Madeleine, there would be a load of people only too happy to fill you in on my activities," Alex murmured.

She took a long drink of coffee, and as her eyes fluttered in pleasure, she forgot all about the bed beneath her.

∞ ∞ ∞

She pulled her cardigan tighter around her body as she approached the kitchen. The sound of laughter and music had met her almost from the bottom step of the stairs, the noise grew louder as she approached the kitchen. She paused in the doorway smiling as Jessica sat on the counter beside the cooker wriggling in her seven-year-old version of dancing. The child was dressed in Maddie's hooded top. The arms were rolled up so her hands, that were creating shapes in the air, were free. Maddie was standing with her back to her. Now dressed in just her PJ bottoms and a white tank top, her hips were shaking in time to the music blasting from the iPad.

"You're making them wrong," Jessica yelled over the noise, looking down at the pan.

"What do you mean? They're perfect!" Maddie replied defensively. She was of good Italian stock and prided herself on her cooking ability, and her French toast was a particular specialty.

"There're no black bits. There're supposed to be black bits. Those are the best bits," Jessica said emphatically. She looked up and caught sight of her mom watching them. "Tell her, Mama, there're supposed to be black bits."

Alex rolled her eyes and entered the kitchen. She placed her cup down beside her daughter and took her face in her hands landing a sloppy kiss on her cheek. "Way to let the doctor know that I burn French toast munchkin," she said regarding her daughter and ignoring the chortle coming from Maddie who was still dancing in front of the cooker.

"But the black bits are the bits I like," Jessica added.

"Okay, how's that?" Maddie asked, tipping the pan towards Jessica to show her the now blackened pieces of French toast.

"Perfect!" The girl clapped her hands together.

"Go sit at the table," Alex instructed, lifting her daughter from the counter. "Is there anything I can help with?" she asked Maddie, using all of her self-control to look into the doctor's brown eyes and not at her chest.

"Grab those plates?" Maddie replied, jerking her head in the direction of the white plates stacked on the counter.

Alex picked them up and took them to the table where Jessica was already kneeling on a chair, knife, and fork at the ready. She put the plates out then sat down giving Jessica a quick glare to remind her of her table manners. The child carefully put down the knife and fork and waited patiently. Alex had just picked up her glass of orange juice and was taking a drink when Maddie started to dish out the slices of French toast from the pan. The movement made her braless breasts move beneath her white top. Alex choked slightly at the sight, and the noise echoed into the glass at her mouth.

"You okay?" Maddie asked concerned.

Managing to drag her eyes northwards Alex gave her a weak smile. "I'm fine, thanks." She puffed air out of the side of her mouth silently berating herself. She was getting as bad as Matt.

They ate breakfast together, chatting about Jessica's day at school. Alex was relieved that she managed, for the most part, to maintain eye-to-eye contact instead of eye-to-nipple. Afterwards, Maddie waved away any offer of help to clear up, and Alex and Jessica left her with a grateful hug and a wave as they made their way back to their home to get ready for the day. Watching them disappear through the gate and reappear on the other side Maddie took a deep breath.

"Okay. Now time to go be a town doctor. How the hell d'you do that?"

She mused over her decision as she stripped her sleepwear off. The bravado and adrenalin from the night before were gone, and in the cold light of day, Maddie was starting to panic about her choice. She had spoken to Timothy again via phone call after Alex and Jessica had left, and agreed to meet him at the clinic where the equipment would be returned to.

She stepped into the shower and switched on the hot water faucet. She gasped as her body was met with a cold stream of water.

"Great. No hot water. Fantastic."

She shivered as she tried to wash her body with the least amount of contact with the water as possible.

∞ ∞ ∞

Lou was sitting behind the counter of Ruby's Coffee Shop. Her mind focused on a 'killer game' of Sudoku, while Alex was in the kitchen preparing pastries. The bell above the door jangled, indicating a customer and she reluctantly laid the puzzle down. Her eyes hovered on it before looking up at the waiting patron. She smiled at Maddie.

"Hey, Doc. What can I getcha?" she asked.

"Hi, can I have a regular skinny Americano with an extra shot, to go, please?"

Lou looked at her in confusion. "I'm sorry what?" she asked, as her hands started to flap in excitement. "You just ordered coffee like they do on TV!" she gushed. "Ohmygod." She looked up at the ceiling as she tried to decipher Maddie's order. "Okay. We do coffee, black or white, and where you gotta go? You just got here."

Opening her mouth to speak, Maddie shook her head. "White coffee is fine, and I have an appointment that I need to get to."

Nodding, Lou frowned. "Okay, white coffee I can do and oh"— She started towards the kitchen, turning back towards Maddie— "wait here." She ran into the kitchen, ignoring a bemused Alex who was kneading dough, and rummaged around in the cupboards. Finally locating what she was looking for she held it aloft triumphantly.

"Where you going with that?" Alex asked curiously.

"Doc wants coffee to go," Lou responded, slipping out of the kitchen.

Alex snorted and put down the dough she had in her hands. She walked to the kitchen door wiping her hands on a towel and pushed the door ajar, but was unable to see past Lou who was busy pouring Maddie's coffee. When the younger woman moved, Alex could see the doctor standing at the shop's window looking out into the street.

"Tada," Lou announced.

As Maddie spun around, her mouth fell open at the orange tippy cup in Lou's hand. "Whaa?" she uttered pointing at the child's cup.

Lou shrugged placing the plastic cup on the counter. "I can't give you a cup to go. So this here is the next best thing. It was Jessica's."

Alex stuffed the towel into her mouth to stop her laughter being heard by the two women. They were looking at each other; one with pride at her problem-solving abilities, the other in complete bemusement at the resultant solution.

"Fine." Maddie rolled her eyes as her lips pulled into a petulant pout. "How much?"

"Ummm." Lou turned back towards the kitchen unsure of how much to charge for a tippy cup of coffee. She caught Alex standing in the doorway a towel in her mouth waving her hands. "On the house." Lou smiled as she turned back to face Maddie who picked the cup up by the handle, and nodded in thanks.

"Have a nice day," Lou shouted as Maddie opened the door, getting a half smile in response.

The door to the shop had barely closed when Lou heard an explosion of laughter behind her coming from the kitchen.

"What?" she asked shrugging.

Maddie stood at the door of the clinic. She held a clipboard and her tippy cup of coffee in one hand and a pen in the other as she checked the items being carried into the building off the list.

"You Doctor Marinelli?"

Maddie looked up from the list towards the voice, having to lower her eyes until she reached the small black woman standing in front of her.

"Yes, I am." Maddie smiled warmly. Before she could enquire who she was speaking with, she realized the small woman was looking her up and down.

"Mmmmmmm," she hummed, apparently done assessing Maddie. "McNeil inside?" the woman asked with a look of disinterest as she brushed past Maddie and entered the clinic.

Maddie watched as she disappeared into the building. "Just go right in," she said, as she shifted the contents of her hands so she could take a drink of coffee.

Ten minutes later, after everything had been removed from the delivery van, Maddie entered the building. She headed towards the sound of laughter coming from one of the examination rooms and hovered uncertainly in the doorway.

"Ah, Doctor Marinelli. This is Marion Mack. Known as Mack to one and all and your nurse. Mack was my nurse for nearly twelve years she knows every ailment this town has." McNeil smiled at the two women.

"Nice to meet you," Maddie said, knowing from experience that having a good relationship with a nurse could mean the difference between an easy or *really* hard experience. "It will be good working with you."

"Hmm," Mack replied noncommittally. "I'm just pleased I don't have to do the commute to St Anton." She thrust a large cell phone towards Maddie who accepted it with a curious look.

"What's this?" she asked, inspecting the ancient looking phone.

"Think on it like the bat phone...when that rings, Gotham needs you," Mack answered. Her eyes narrowed and her lips puckered. "If it rings, it's me on the other end, an' you better come running." She swept out of room intent on getting the clinic back in order.

Timothy let out a nervous chuckle. "She's a pussycat really." He changed the subject quickly when he saw Maddie's raised eyebrow in response as she sat down on the examination table beside him. "So I spoke to the chief over at St Anton. Though you've not done a family medicine residency, they're going to allow you to practice under their insurance thanks to the ER hours you've clocked up. They called Atlanta General this morning and spoke to the Chief of Staff there. However, we appreciate that this isn't your area of expertise so I will be available for consultancy if you need it, and you can call St Anton's and speak to any doc there as well. This time of year it's mostly allergies." He gave her a supportive smile and patted her leg as he stood up and left the room.

Maddie looked somewhat relieved at hearing that as, after her proclamation during the night, panic had set in that she'd got herself in over her head, and it had been mounting throughout the morning. Timothy poked his head back around the corner of the door.

"Oh, and snake bites," he added smiling, before disappearing again as Maddie flopped back onto the examination table groaning.

"You planning on laying there all day?" Mack's voice came from the doorway. "'cause there's a waiting room full of people."

"What?" Maddie exclaimed. "Jesus, word goes fast around here."

"They're here to give you a test drive, buckle up, Doctor Marinelli." Mack half smiled. "An' lose the tippy cup," she remarked as Maddie stood up.

The doctor looked down at the plastic cup still in her hand and rolled her eyes. She walked around to take a seat behind the desk and opened a drawer, letting the cup fall into it before slamming it closed with a flourish. She plastered a welcoming smile on her face ready to meet her first patient of the day.

"Okay, who's first?" she called.

∞ ∞ ∞

Letting her head fall onto the desk Maddie exhaled. When Grace Falls decides to test drive a doctor, they do not hold back. She'd had a steady stream of patients all day and was proud that she had only had to call for consults on a couple of occasions. Her brain was frazzled though after trawling through her memory banks for seldom-used information throughout the day.

"Good night, Doctor Marinelli," Mack called from the hallway, switching off the lights in the other rooms as she went.

"Goodnight, Mack," she shouted. "Have a lovely evening. See you tomorrow."

"So you're coming back then?"

Maddie lifted her head from the desk at the sound of a different voice from the one she had expected.

Alex smiled pushing herself off from the doorframe where she had taken a moment to watch the exhausted doctor. She walked forward and placed a silver travel mug in front of Maddie on the desk.

"One skinny Americano with an extra shot, to go."

"But I really preferred the tippy cup." Maddie gestured lifting the orange plastic cup from her open drawer. She took a sip from the silver mug and groaned with pleasure. "I could get used to finishing work like this." She smiled. "The coffee I mean." Her eyes twinkled as Alex flushed slightly while recalling their conversation from the morning.

Alex coughed and let her eyes wander around the room. "I wondered whether you wanted to come over for dinner tonight. It's Matt's night with Jessica, and I wanted to thank you properly for what you did," she said, starting to move back towards the door. "And apologize if we in some way prompted you to give up your vacation for this." She leaned nonchalantly on the balance beam scales beside the door.

"Spending the night in a steamy bathroom with you and Jessica was in part responsible for my decision," Maddie said tidying her desk and standing up, missing Alex's less than graceful slide as she placed too much pressure on the balance scales at Maddie's mention of steamy bathrooms. "I would never have forgiven myself if something had happened to her. So no thank you or apology is necessary. However, dinner sounds divine," Maddie said, suddenly aware of how hungry she was.

Recovering her composure, Alex grinned and turned into the hall of the medical clinic. "Remember that whatever I cook, the black bits are the best."

∞ ∞ ∞

"So how was your first day?" Alex asked as they walked through the town towards their homes.

Maddie let out a long breath. "Busy, yup, busy would describe it." She gave Alex a tired smile.

Alex laughed. "And I bet you quite eventful! Let's see, day one you will have had Mrs. Hayes, who's never had a sick day in her life but would have sat there almost daring you to find something wrong with her." She looked at Maddie who looked back in astonishment. Alex took the look as confirmation and chuckled before continuing with her assessment of Maddie's day. "And you would have had old man Jackson in with his huge testicle." She raised an eyebrow towards the doctor.

"Okay, how?" Maddie started to ask, before stopping herself out of concern about patient confidentiality. She laughed and shook her head in surprise at the accuracy of Alex's predictions.

"Don't worry, you didn't give anything away. There are no secrets in Grace Falls remember. Mrs. Hayes has been goading doctors for years into finding something wrong with her. The old bird is stronger than an ox and, as far as I know, has never even had a cold. And as for Old man Jackson, well, every male in his family has one huge testicle, and between you and me, I am not convinced that some of the females don't either. For the record, I have never seen any generation of Jackson testicle. I'm just going on hearsay plus my grandma was Mack before Mack was Mack." Alex smiled.

Maddie nodded slowly. "She was the town nurse?" she asked cautiously, hoping she'd followed Alex correctly.

"There're entire generations in Grace Falls where the first hands to touch them when they came into this world were my grandma's. She used to take great pleasure in giving Matt and Peter a cuff around the ear telling them that her hands were the first to hold them and she'd be the first to smack 'em if they got out of line." Alex smiled thinking about the small, formidable woman who was wholly adored by everyone in the town. She paused thinking about who else might appear in Maddie's surgery. A scowl appeared on her face as a face popped into her mind. "If Virginia Grace comes in don't take anything that she says personally. The woman is a first class bitch and has been ever since I've known her. I don't blame Charlotte for getting the hell out of here. If Virginia was my mother, you wouldn't see me for dust. Grandma used to take great joy in taking her down a peg or two. I think there was probably more than one occasion where she gave Virginia a laxative just 'cause 'that woman don't seem to think her shit smells the same as the rest of us.'" Alex said mimicking her grandmother's strong accent.

"Duly noted," Maddie said with a grin. "I will have laxatives at the ready."

"Oh, has Emmet Day been in yet?" Alex asked excitedly.

Wracking her brain, Maddie tried to place the name. Slowly she shook her head unable to recall the name from the countless people she had seen.

"He'll be in tomorrow. He lives farther out of town so getting in isn't always easy for him. Emmet's a hypochondriac. He got given a book a few years back of illness and ailments, he's working his way through it." Alex screwed her face up in thought. "I think we're up to e."

Before Maddie could respond, the doctor's attention was caught by a swishing sound behind them. She turned, and her jaw went slack as Sam moved towards them. His feet were attached to long skis with wheels along the bottom, and his arms pumped the poles in his hands furiously against the concrete to aid his propulsion.

"Hey, Sam." Alex waved cheerily at the mechanic.

"Alex, Doc. How's it goin'?" Sam yelled as he spun past them.

"Good," Alex yelled at his back, she cupped her hands against her mouth. "Looking good, Sam," she shouted. The man held up one pole in response without looking back.

Maddie looked at Alex and the departing Sam unable to decide where to begin with her questions about what she had just seen. Eventually, she pointed in the direction where Sam had skated. "What was that?"

Alex looked at the doctor and then towards where she was pointing. "Sam? He's training, he wants to get into the Olympic cross-country skiing squad," she answered as if it were the most natural thing in the world.

Still looking into the now empty distance, Maddie frowned. "Do you get much snow here?"

Grinning Alex shook her head. "Nope, never even seen a single flake here. He's not got a hope in hell, but he loves trying. Last year it was the luge."

"Apart from the lack of ice, you don't have any hills," Maddie said slowly. "At least I haven't seen any."

"Nope." Alex laughed. "We don't which is why he switched to skiing. Last year after his sister Erin told him 'no damn way' he persuaded Matt to tow him from his truck. All was going well until Matt braked and the luge and Sam didn't. He shot under the truck, but then the rope ran out so the luge stopped but Sam didn't. Doc McNeil was picking grit out his back and ass for weeks, and Erin chewed his and Matt's butts off for about the same time." She caught sight of Maddie's incredulous look. "Don't worry, for the most part we're a sane bunch."

They stopped as they reached the point in the road where they would separate to go to their respective homes. "I'll just grab a quick shower, hot water depending and come over if that's okay?" Maddie asked.

"If you've no hot water come over, you can shower at mine." There was a brief pause before Alex added hastily. "It's only fair since I'm the reason why you don't have any."

"Thanks, I'll see you in a bit." Maddie smiled and headed towards the Anderson house partly hoping that the hot water hadn't replenished as the more time she spent with Alex, the more time she wanted.

Ten minutes later and Maddie stood at the back door of Alex's home, twisting the bag she held in her hand, which contained a change of clothes, a towel, Mack's brick of a cell phone, and her wash bag.

Alex opened the door and looked at the doctor still dressed as she had been when she had left her. "No water?"

"No water," Maddie confirmed.

Alex let the door open fully to allow Maddie to enter. She showed her up to the bathroom and left her to shower. Returning back downstairs she tried to concentrate on not chopping a digit off in preparing dinner while trying not to think about Maddie naked in her shower upstairs.

Maddie stepped out of the shower and dried quickly. She was desperate not to waste any time when she could be downstairs talking with Alex, watching her smile and hearing the delicious sound of her laughter. She checked herself in the mirror as she ran a hand through her damp locks to fluff them up. "Relax, Maddie, she's not interested," she murmured to her reflection.

Entering the kitchen, where Alex was adding chopped peppers to a wok, Maddie took a moment to take in the warm, inviting room. She smiled at Jessica's drawings pinned to the fridge.

"Oh hey."Alex smiled turning to face her. "I have white and red. I wasn't sure what you'd prefer." She wiped her hands on the cloth tucked into the pocket of her jeans and held up two bottles of wine.

"Red please, but a small glass, in case I get called." Maddie smiled slipping onto a stool at the breakfast bar. "Can I help?"

"Nope, burning is all under control thanks," Alex replied pouring a small glass of wine and handing it across. "I am sorry that your vacation is now being spent looking at the moles and bunions of Grace Falls." She flashed Maddie a sympathetic smile before turning back to stir the contents of the wok. "Nothing fancy just chicken and vegetable," she called over her shoulder.

"Sounds perfect," Maddie responded, sipping her wine and feeling completely relaxed and at home. She looked around the room her eyes stopping on a town sign with the population number on it. "Did you steal that?"

Alex turned around to look to where Maddie was pointing. "Oh that, no. It's tradition here. When you give birth, they give you a copy of the town sign with the population increased by one. That's Jessica's." She returned her attention to the cooker.

Maddie spun around on the chair to focus her attention on Alex. "It must have been difficult...Jessica being so premature."

"God, this town! Who told you? What else do you know?" Alex replied, her tone harsher than she intended.

"No-one. Nothing. Jessica said that Doctor McNeil called her two pounds of stubborn, so I assumed. I'm sorry," Maddie said quickly.

Closing her eyes Alex exhaled. "No it's me, I'm sorry." She shook her head. "This place can be terrible for gossip and with the situation between Matt, me and Jessica we get our fair share." She switched off the gas ring and tipped the food onto two plates. "It was hard, yes." She looked at the ceiling and shook her head shaking the memory of that time from her mind. "Mack and Timothy are the only reason that she's still here." She handed over a plate and placed her own down on the breakfast bar, and then turned to collect cutlery from the drawer.

Maddie accepted the plate of food and put it on the counter in front of her, waiting for Alex to pass cutlery. "I can't imagine how you coped," she said with a soft smile.

"So, you know a lot about me and my family, such as it is, Doctor Marinelli. While you remain a mystery, enigmatic, and intriguing."

Laughing as she poked a fork through her food Maddie raised her eyebrows and replied in a teasing tone. "Enigmatic and intriguing, huh. I'm going to add that to the gorgeous of last night. I'm getting quite a collection of adjectives from you, Ms. Milne. Especially if I add...I believe it was, hot, on the list."

Alex choked on a piece of pepper. "Who told you that?" she exclaimed while gulping down some wine to clear her throat.

"Sully," they both said at once.

"I will kill him," Alex muttered.

Maddie started to eat. "Mmm this is delicious," she said eagerly taking another mouthful. "I have a question for you. How come you call Sully, Matt, won't let anyone shorten Jessica's name and call me Madeline. Yet you call Teddy, Teddy, and your brother Bear, when all the while you yourself have a shortened name?"

Alex chuckled. "What can I say? I'm contrary, and you're trying to avoid talking about yourself."

"So what would you like to know?"

Alex played with the stem of her wine glass. "Where're you from? Family? What you running from?"

Maddie looked up abruptly at the last question. "What makes you think I'm running?"

"I've seen the look before," she replied sadly, focusing on her food.

Maddie's eyes narrowed. "Bear?" she asked quietly.

Alex looked up in surprise and let out a soft breath. "Yeahup, Bear," she confirmed.

"Brooklyn, I'm from Brooklyn," Maddie said taking a bite of her food wanting to give Alex the opportunity to change the subject. "I have parents and a brother and sister all still in Brooklyn, and a failed marriage behind me." She cast a glance down at her ring finger, which despite the passage of time still bore a slight indent from the ring that had once resided there.

"Is that why you're moving across the country? A failed marriage?" Alex asked, disguising her disappointment. In light of this new information, any hope she had of Maddie being attracted to women was diminishing, despite the flirtatious vibe she was getting from her.

"I guess. It ended quite brutally, and I grew tired of the pity that I saw in my friends' eyes and living in our home with so many reminders of Jo..." She quickly shortened Joanna's name as she became suddenly anxious about acceptance in such a small town. She was unsure what would happen were she to out herself; even to someone that she instinctively trusted. "We were together for a long time, and I suppose I wanted a clean break and fresh start, and yeah, maybe I'm running. A friend from med school contacted me about a job in San Francisco, and it was a great career opportunity."

Alex ate her meal quietly for a few moments, before looking at Maddie. Her eyes narrowed. "You know I never knew whether Bear was running away from or running towards something. He joined up so young and once he was in the military he couldn't see his life out of it anymore. One of his last letters said that he realized that it was important to know what you're looking for before you set off after it." She gave Maddie a sad smile then stood up to clear their now empty plates leaving Maddie to mull over her words.

Maddie took her empty wine glass across to the sink where Alex stood looking out of the window as she washed the plates clean. Maddie was unsure whether she was looking into the darkness of the night or her reflection mirrored in the kitchen window.

"He was right, it is important," Maddie said, resting her backside against the counter, "and you're the only person that's called me on it. I don't know if I'm running away or towards, only that I needed to run." She shrugged. "Only it appears that I, well my car at least, ran out of steam."

"And I'm grateful for that, 'cause you and your steam saved my little girl." Alex smiled and nodded emphatically as she placed the washed glasses onto the drainer. "You like what I did there?" She grinned.

"Yeah, neat segue." Maddie laughed reaching for the towel to dry the dishes draining beside the sink. She looked up in surprise as Alex snatched the towel from her grasp. "Hey!"

"You're a guest, no helping," Alex chastised.

"Alex, you cooked. You've been working in the coffee shop all day, let me at least dry the dishes," Maddie said, attempting to take the towel out of Alex's hand.

"Nope!" Alex put her hand behind her back and held a finger up to rebuke Maddie.

Maddie lunged for the towel trapping Alex between her body and the counter. "Seriously give me the towel."

She tried to snatch the towel from Alex's now raised arm, which was waving back and forth out of Maddie's reach. Their laughter mingled until Maddie managed to grab the towel. Suddenly, both women became aware of the closeness of their faces as their bodies pressed against each other.

Maddie swallowed hard as she looked into Alex's eyes. Her lips opened, moving as if about to speak. Her eyes switched to look at Alex's mouth, which was open and inviting. She had almost made up her mind to give in and kiss the enticing lips when the sound of a tinny version of American Pie disturbed the moment.

"What's that?" Maddie breathed.

"I, I don't know," Alex said quietly. "I think it's coming from your bag."

"Shit. The bat phone," Maddie gasped, throwing the towel down onto the counter and turning away from Alex; who let out a long breath as her entire body dropped a couple of inches without the warmth of Maddie against her.

Maddie rummaged through the bag until she located the brick of a cell phone that Mack had foisted on her.

"Hello?" she said answering the call. She listened for a moment. "Okay, I'll be right there." She gave Alex an apologetic look. "I'm sorry. I have to..." She indicated over her shoulder with her thumb.

"No, no it's okay, go!" Alex replied, having regained some modicum of composure during Maddie's quick call. She hustled Maddie through the house and opened the front door. Holding onto the thick wooden door for support, she watched Maddie's hurried exit.

"Thanks for dinner," Maddie yelled, as she sprinted from the house.

"You're welcome," Alex replied, watching as Maddie ran towards the clinic.

∞ ∞ ∞

She arrived sweating and out of breath at the door of the clinic, only to be greeted by a casually dressed Mack.

"You ran here?" Mack asked, looking up and down the street for a car. "Where's your car?"

"If I had a car I wouldn't be in Grace Falls, I'd be well on my way to San Francisco by now," Maddie replied, trying to catch her breath. "What do we have?" she asked, walking into the clinic.

"Parents are bringing in a ten-month-old. Severe fever and vomiting," Mack responded while holding out a white coat for Maddie to slip on.

She spent the next two hours in the company of two frantic first-time parents and a screaming child with an ear infection and a seemingly amazing ability to resist all the pain relief that she could safely give him. The screeching finally subsided when his eardrum perforated, and he lay in his mother's arms whimpering. Happy that his temperature was dropping Maddie wrote them a prescription for more painkillers and antibiotics and gave them instructions to come back to see her in a few days. She was showing them out when Timothy's words about treating the people, not the illness came back to her.

"Why don't you leave him with me here for an hour or so while he's quiet and sleeping and you two go take a walk around the block or something. Just get some peace and quiet."

The young couple looked at her with tired eyes.

She gave them a warm smile. "It can be tough when you've listened to your child in pain. Give yourselves a break, even for ten minutes."

They gave her a grateful nod and walked out to get a moment's respite in the cooling evening.

"Whaat?" Maddie asked, turning around with the sleeping baby in her arms, seeing Mack standing watching her.

"Didn't say a thing," the nurse replied, walking into the office.

Chapter Three

The next morning Maddie woke up feeling invigorated; the two parents had come back twenty minutes later after she had sent them off. Both had looked much brighter after taking just a few moments for themselves. The young mum kept hugging Maddie and thanking her profusely before they drove off.

She had managed to skillfully avoid thinking about the moment with Alex the previous evening, deciding that avoidance was the best policy to stop her groaning with embarrassment at her practically pinning the poor woman against her cupboards and almost kissing her. She showered, dressed, and stepped out into the warm morning, frowning at the vehicle parked on the street outside her front gate.

"What the?" she said aloud.

"Mack said we needed to give you a courtesy vehicle while we're fixing your car."

Maddie jumped and clutched her chest turning to look at Sam who was sitting on the porch swing.

"Something about it not being right having a doctor running through town in her high tops to treat people." He shrugged.

"So you got me a golf cart?" Maddie asked, her eyes wide with incredulity.

"Best we could do at short notice, and Mack said we had to have it here first thing"—Sam stood up and handed Maddie a key—"an' no-one messes with Mack." He jumped off the step and started walking down the pathway.

"Can I give you a ride?" Maddie called after him.

He turned and grinned at her. "Nope, bad enough I had to ride it here!"

Maddie glowered at him. "Fix my damn car!" she yelled.

The mechanic waved his hand above his head without turning around, earning a low growl from the frustrated doctor.

"Two weeks," he shouted back.

"And a half, tops, I know," Maddie finished, muttering as she approached the golf cart.

∞ ∞ ∞

She pulled up to the clinic and parked the golf cart outside, scowling as Mack came out of the door to greet her.

"What the hell is that?" the small nurse asked, handing Maddie a cup of coffee.

"My courtesy vehicle," Maddie grumbled taking the coffee and walking past her into the clinic.

"I will kick Campbell's ass up and down this town," Mack muttered. "I told him a car!" she shouted after Maddie as she followed her into the building.

Maddie pulled on her white coat. "That's apparently the closest thing they had. So what have we got on the pad for today?" she asked, giving an over-exaggerated shudder to release the tension from her transport woes.

"We have Emmett Day coming in first thing."

"Book guy?" Maddie asked, remembering Alex's comments as they walked home.

"That's him! How'd you know? Oh, wait, you had dinner with Alex last night." Mack grinned. Ignoring Maddie's muttered 'Jesus have they tagged me or something?' She scurried after the tall doctor as she entered the examination room. "An' tonight you have the radio clinic."

Maddie stopped abruptly causing the nurse to run into the back of her. "I have the what...?"

"The radio clinic. We have a lot of folks who struggle to get into town, so we started a clinic on the airwaves." Mack swept her hand through the air enthusiastically, proud of the service that she had started. "They call in, and you offer advice over the CB."

"No! Not happening," Maddie said, sitting down behind the desk and putting her coffee cup down. "Anyone could be listening in to what should be a private discussion with a doctor."

Mack narrowed her eyes and leaned on the desk. "Everyone knows the deal. If it's important or they don't want anything to be public knowledge they come into town or get a home visit. This way when it's little things they get medical advice. It's a valuable service."

Maddie looked up shrinking back slightly at the glare she was receiving from the small nurse. "I...I..." she spluttered. "I'll think about it," she said, reaching for her coffee which Mack slipped out of her reach.

"Hmm?" Mack said unimpressed.

"Really?" Maddie looked at Mack and her now distant coffee cup. "Fine, I'll do it." She groaned at a smiling Mack, who pushed the cup back towards her.

∞ ∞ ∞

"For the fifth time, Mr. Day, you don't have endometriosis," Maddie sighed. Her fingers flexed in frustration. She pushed them together and pressed them against her lips, to stop them reaching out to strangle the man sitting opposite her.

"And I'm saying you can't be sure of that," the man said crossing his arms and leaning back in the seat.

"I can," Maddie almost yelled. What little patience she had with Emmett Day and his book of ailments had worn thin to the point of a sliver. She took a deep breath to compose herself. "I can be sure because you. Are. *Not.* A. Woman," she said slowly, emphasizing each word.

"You're sure about that?" Emmett asked.

Maddie's eyes widened, and she held her hands up in defeat. She pushed her chair back from the desk. "Okay, Mr. Day, we both know you don't have endometriosis. We both also know that you are slowly working your way through whatever medical book you have." She pulled on a pair of rubber gloves snapping them into place. "So, we can do this one of two ways. One, I skip a couple of entries and introduce you to enema." She smiled as she over-enunciated the final word.

The patient's brow furrowed as she walked slowly towards him.

"Or two, I can do a full work up on you and see whether we can find something actually wrong with you, and I won't rest until I find even the tiniest mole that looks suspicious. So which option is it to be, Mr. Day?" she asked ominously keeping a smile plastered on her face.

"Option two please, Doc," he replied facing forward, giving her a sidelong look.

"Excellent, but seriously, Mr. Day, I will do this work up, and I will do a full exam every day on you while I'm here if that's what it takes, but you have *got* to lose the book." Maddie perched onto the desk and gave his arm a reassuring rub.

Emmet smiled shyly. Finally raising his eyes to meet Maddie's he nodded slowly.

"Okay...I'll try," he said quietly.

"Alrighty then, let's get some blood work done," Maddie said brightly, moving across the room to get supplies.

∞ ∞ ∞

"Did I miss it?" Alex asked, lifting Jessica onto the bar before shrugging her jacket off and sitting on the stool beside Teddy.

"Not yet," Teddy replied, blowing a loud raspberry on a giggling Jessica's cheek before resuming her position at the bar leaning forward so she could hear the radio better.

Alex waved across to Sully who was approaching with a wide smile on his face that was reserved for his daughter. "How's my favorite girl?" he said scooping Jessica off the bar and into the air, holding her aloft above his head. "No more asthma attacks?"

"Daddy, put me down," Jessica giggled.

"Awwww nope, I'm going to keep you up there and serve all my customers with you just hovering up there." Sully laughed rolling his daughter back and forth.

Screwing her face up Alex looked at her friend and their daughter. "She's just eaten, Matt, she'll barf on your head again."

Sully looked over towards Alex then back up at his daughter, recalling the many times that his daughter's stomach had not coped with rambunctious play. He nodded and brought Jessica down into a hug.

"Don't want that, do we, sport." He laughed, plunking her back down onto the spot on the bar where she had sat from the first time she was allowed out of the hospital. On that day Sully had proudly sat her car seat on the bar for all and sundry to come see her while warning them not to breathe beer fumes over his pride and joy. He opened a bottle of beer and passed it to Alex.

"How's she doing?" Alex asked pointing her beer bottle towards the radio. "I can't believe she agreed to do it."

Ruth slid the nuts along the bar towards Alex. "Are you kidding? She was dealing with Mack. She never stood a chance."

There were murmurs of agreement as they each considered when they had been faced with Mack.

"Anything good so far? God, I can't believe how much I'd missed this." Alex smiled, popping a handful of nuts into her mouth.

"So far, one swollen knee, Sammy Dale has a bad case of thrush, made worse by her putting athlete's foot cream on it, and Lucy Simpson has tonsillitis," Sully replied piercing the straw into a carton of orange juice and handing it to Jessica. "She had to write notes for Steve to read out to the doc." He smiled. "And the doc is doing good, she has a voice for radio, and a body for—"

"Matt!" Alex interrupted him with a warning glare, indicating her head towards Jessica.

He grinned as he placed his hands over his daughter's ears. Jessica glanced up toward her father while continuing to suck juice through her straw.

"Don't pretend you haven't thought about it," he joked.

Teddy looked at Alex with raised eyebrows, waiting for her to answer. Before Alex could respond there was a roar from the bar.

"Everybody quiet, here it is," Peter shouted standing up on the footrest of the stool waving his arms to shush everyone.

"Hi, Mr. White, thanks for calling in." Maddie's voice filled the bar.

Alex couldn't help but smile at how right Sully was about her voice and her body.

"What can I do for you?"

"Here it comes," Teddy murmured under her breath, earning a glare from Peter to be quiet as he sat listening while staring intently at his watch.

"Well, Doctor, I have some...protrusions."

There was a series of snorts of laughter across the bar, followed by various shushing sounds.

"Okay." Maddie's tone sounded wary but concerned. "What kind of protrusions?"

"Painful ones."

The bar was deathly quiet apart from the noise of sucking coming from Jessica and her now empty carton of orange juice, which Alex gently extricated from her daughter before she got lynched.

"Okay, where exactly are these protrusions?" Maddie asked.

There was the sound of movement coming from the radio and muffled voices. Everyone in the bar leaned forward towards the radio.

"How many times, Gregor White have I told you, and that sorry ass of yours, to come in?" Mack's voice rang throughout the bar.

"One minute five seconds," Peter yelled.

Mack's voice continued to blast from the radio. "Those protrusions are hemorrhoids. Hemorrhoids," she repeated emphasizing each syllable loudly. "You stupid man and if you'd come into town like I've been at you to do for almost a year we could do something for them," she continued to rant.

Sully checked the chalkboard behind the bar. "Ruth wins!" he exclaimed. "She had one minute four."

Ruth held her hands above her head in victory, accepting the basket of money Sully passed her. She scoped the notes out of the basket and began to tidy them into a neat pile. "I thank you all," she shouted above the groans of disappointment from the other bar-goers at losing the 'how long 'til Mack loses it with Gregor White sweepstake,' which had become a regular Friday night activity in Grace Falls when the radio clinic was in full swing.

"Sooo," Teddy said, swinging around to face Alex. "Now that I'm down ten bucks, how 'bout we shoot, and I drink your liquor cabinet dry?"

Alex drained her beer. "And people wonder why I worry about my child's education when you come out with things like that!" She laughed.

"Miss Roosevelt is my favorite teacher ever," Jessica said earnestly, looking for her aunt's approval, and getting a wink in response.

"And the only teacher you've ever had. Say bye to your daddy," Alex replied giving Teddy a playful slap for brainwashing her child.

"Bye, Daddy," Jessica called, holding her hand up, and blowing kisses towards her father.

Sully grinned and reached up pretending to catch them.

"Bye, sweetie, see you tomorrow," he shouted, reaching around to switch the radio off and the music back on.

"Teddy, double or quits remember!" Ruth shouted.

Teddy saluted their friend as she held the door open for Alex and Jessica.

"What was that about?" Alex asked gripping her daughter's hand.

"Nooo idea." Teddy smiled taking Jessica's other hand and preparing to swing her into the air.

∞ ∞ ∞

Maddie had her face planted on the desk. The radio show had been finished for five minutes, and she was yet to raise her head up.

"The fool of a man has been suffering from those for almost two years and has called in on every radio clinic we've had," Mack said, bustling around and tidying up the office around the immobile doctor.

"Doesn't mean you berate him over the airwaves," Maddie said, her voice muffled against the desk.

Mack stopped and looked at Maddie. "You threatened Emmett Day with an enema this morning, you don' get to judge," she said, trying to hide her smile.

Maddie's shoulders started to move as she chuckled.

"You were good, Doc. See there was no reason for all that panic and griping," she added pulling on her jacket.

Maddie raised her head up and gave Mack a sorrowful look. "I have to admit it wasn't as bad as I thought it was going to be," she admitted with a slow smile.

"Well, you were good, have a good evening." Mack gave her a small, proud nod then disappeared. "An' lock up after you," she yelled from the hall.

Maddie sighed. Standing up she switched the light off in the office and walked out, fishing the medical center's keys out of her purse. She locked the door then stepped out into the cooling night air and grimaced at the golf cart parked out front.

"Yeah I'm gonna walk," she said aloud. As she walked through the town, she decided to pay her first visit to Sullivan's Bar. She pushed open the door, and the warmth from the bar hit her along with the sound of laughter and chatter, which immediately stopped as she entered the room. Her eyes opened wide, and she considered turning tail and leaving. But before she could move Sully started to clap. The slow rhythmic clap was soon joined by others, and it picked up pace until it was a full round of applause throughout the bar. Maddie gave an embarrassed wave in response and smiled gratefully as Ruth waved her over towards her.

"What can I getcha, Doc?" Sully asked. "And your money is no good here after what you did for my little girl." He smiled.

"In that case, I'll have whatever is the most expensive," Maddie joked. "Actually I just came in to pick up a bottle of wine?"

"Red or white?" Sully asked.

"Red please, just whatever you've got will be fine," Maddie replied as Sully went off to select a bottle, leaving her with Ruth and Peter.

Ruth turned awkwardly on the stool due to her bulk. "You were great...on the radio clinic," she said.

Maddie blushed slightly. "You heard?" she replied, running her hand through her hair.

"We all did," Peter grinned.

"All?" Maddie started to feel slightly queasy at the thought.

Sully set a bottle wrapped in paper down in front of Maddie. "Yup, it's practically an institution. So all I've been hearing from my daughter is Maddie-Lyn this and Maddie-Lyn that. You appear to have made quite an impression on her."

"She's a lovely kid." Maddie smiled.

"Yeah, she is. Thank God she takes after Alex more than me." He laughed heading off to serve customers further down the bar.

"Any news on the parts for my car?" Maddie asked picking up the bottle.

"Hmmm, nope. Excuse me." Peter quickly slipped off the stool and made a hasty retreat towards the men's room. He was a terrible liar and opted for deflection or avoidance as an approach to dealing with the doctor's queries about her car.

Maddie sucked air through her teeth as she watched him go. She turned to Ruth who had a thoughtful look on her face as she watched her husband disappear.

"So how are you feeling, still no sign of that little one appearing?" Maddie asked.

Ruth looked down at her stomach. "I'm starting to think that it's never going to come out. It could be a race to see what gets here first; the baby or your car parts."

Laughing, Maddie held up the bottle of wine in thanks towards Sully. "Goodnight," she called. She was taken by surprise as almost everyone in the bar responded to her.

∞ ∞ ∞

Alex sat on the porch swing, looking across towards the Anderson house, frowning at the darkness that shrouded it. She was idly wondering where Maddie was when Teddy flopped down onto the seat beside her and handed her a bottle of tequila.

"I have glasses you know." Alex smiled accepting the bottle and taking a swig.

"I know, but this way makes me feel young again," Teddy replied, stretching her legs out in front of her. "So you wanna tell me what's going on with the hot doctor?"

"Nothing," Alex said. Seeing a look of disbelief on her friend's face, she repeated herself. "Nothing!"

Teddy narrowed her eyes. "Hmmm, so is she as hot as manwhore says she is?" she asked as she took the bottle back from Alex and drank slowly from it.

"Hotter and please stop calling Matt that. Jessica's heard you and told Madeleine her daddy was a manhole."

Teddy spluttered forward catching the dribble of tequila that had escaped her mouth with her fingers. "Sorry, I'll stop. Can I still use kidult though?" she asked, once she had composed herself.

Alex snorted. "That I will allow." She took a long drink from the bottle, wincing at the taste. "We should have got lemons," she mused.

"Madeleine?" Teddy remarked raising her eyebrow. "And hotter huh?" she grinned, ignoring Alex's attempt to change the subject.

"Waaay hotter and smart and funny, and *leaving,*" Alex replied, emphasizing the last word in the hope that Teddy would drop it.

Teddy looked at her friend. "Her leaving doesn't mean that you can't have some fun while she's here! Do you think she likes you?"

"I have no idea. I mean, my head says no. She's divorced for God's sake, but I get this vibe from her so my—"

"Crotch says yes?" Teddy finished for her.

Alex slapped her thigh. "I was going to say gaydar."

"Same difference." Teddy laughed. "Isn't that where the antenna is?"

Alex lay her head against the back of the swing. "I found a hair growing out of my nipple when I was in the shower this morning," she said in a thoughtful tone.

Teddy looked at her wondering where this was going, before mirroring her friend's pose. "I've had that," she replied, hoping to make her friend feel better.

"It's not that it was there, it was more how long it was." She held up her thumb and forefinger to her friend to illustrate.

Teddy let out a low whistle.

"Do you know how long since someone has seen my boobs? How long it's been since someone has looked at my fun bits?" Alex asked sadly.

Teddy cradled the tequila bottle between her thighs. "Mack, eight months ago," she said, glancing at Alex with a smirk on her face.

"Pap tests don't count," Alex groaned sitting back upright.

"If it doesn't count, how come you vajazzled for her?!"

Alex snatched the bottle from between Teddy's thighs. "I did not vajazzle, I groomed. I just didn't realize that the stupid soap you'd gotten Jessica had glitter in it!"

Teddy gave a soft snort. "Okay, so it's been a while. As much as this is going to pain me, why don't you give the vet another go?"

"Erin?" Alex said, surprised that Teddy had brought her up. "You still can't bring yourself to say her name can you?" She laughed when she saw Teddy's scowl. "Jeez, you hold a grudge. It was over twenty years ago."

"That ball was out and Erin Hunter, see I can say her name." Teddy scrunched her nose up in distaste. "She knew it was out and she said nothing, and I lost that match to Charlotte Grace. Wait, wasn't it

Charlotte Grace that you almost banged on Ruth's mama's bed that time?" she said. Her eyes widened as a thought came to her.

"Why are you dredging this up?"

"Do you think she had a crush on Charlotte and that's why she said the ball was in?" Teddy narrowed her eyes as she considered her new theory on why she had lost the county's tennis title.

"Over twenty years, Teddy, let it go," Alex said, suppressing a laugh. Even after all these years, Teddy was still oblivious to what had happened between Charlotte and Erin. However, Alex had to admit that she was only aware of it after Erin confided in her and with hindsight she was astounded that she had missed all the signals. "Whether Erin had a crush on Charlotte twenty years ago is neither here nor there and don't let Sam hear you saying that about his sister, you know how he feels about the Grace family."

Teddy huffed. "Okay so putting her tennis cheating ways to the side, why don't you give her another go?"

Alex thought back to the few dates she'd had with the local vet and gave her friend a rueful smile. "Well apart from her going to Auburn, which would mean no watching the Iron Bowl ever, and your inability to forget her minor line calling indiscretion twenty years ago." She held her hand up as Teddy was about to interject. As much as she loved seeing Teddy in righteous indignation mode, she wasn't up for it tonight. "I guess when I eventually ignored Sam giving me the evil eye for dating his big sister, I found that she's still a really lovely woman, and I enjoyed spending time with her but there just wasn't a—"

"Party in your pants?" Teddy supplied with a wicked grin.

"I was going with a spark."

"Which is why if your crotch is tweaking now you should at least go for it."

"I like her. I mean I'm stupidly attracted to her, but I want a relationship with someone. Someone to bring me coffee in bed in the morning, not just a random hump." Alex sighed taking another swig from the bottle. "Although it is a bit like having a superpower and not being able to use it." She let out a long frustrated growl.

"Seriously, a superpower!" Teddy laughed. "So why don't you try and find out if your vajaydar is right?"

A light went on in the kitchen of the Anderson house.

"Maybe." Alex smiled.

Chapter Four

Maddie yawned and checked the clock. The banging at her front door that had woken her up continued unabated.

"Please don't let this be a sick person," she muttered sleepily, swinging her legs around and grabbing her hoodie. She padded down the stairs rubbing her eyes and blinking at the sunlight streaming in through the windows either side of her front door. She yanked open the door fully expecting to see an anxious face needing her help on the other side. Instead, she was looking at Peter who was nervously gazing downward as he shuffled from foot to foot. He raised his head welcoming Maddie with a broad smile.

"Morning!" he said cheerfully.

"Is it Ruth? Is she okay?" Maddie asked, turning to pick up her bag, which now habitually sat beside the front door.

Peter held his hands out in front of him and shook his head. "No, no, nothing like that. I felt bad"—he gave her a sheepish look—"about the golf cart, so I thought you could use this instead." He moved out of the way to allow Maddie to see the cherry red T-Bird that he had restored.

"Wow," Maddie said in awe. Ignoring her bare feet, she brushed past Peter and walked in wonder towards the car. "This was the one you worked on?" she asked over her shoulder.

"For almost a year," Peter said proudly.

Maddie walked around Peter's prized possession taking in the faultless paint job. The chrome bumpers reflected the hazy morning sunshine.

"She's beautiful."

"An' she's yours"—Peter replied holding out a set of keys—"until we get yours up and running."

Her eyes widened as she looked at the mechanic and the car. "Really?" she asked cautiously, before grinning as Peter nodded. Maddie broke into a wide smile as she took the keys from Peter and climbed into the driver's seat. She allowed her hands to run over the soft leather of the interior. "You have done a remarkable job on her," she said ducking her head out of the window to look at Peter.

Peter shrugged, "When you love doing something it's not work. Anyway, I should get going." He gave the car a fond pat. "Just don't drive her like you did yours," he warned.

Maddie gave him a bashful smile as she caressed the steering wheel. "I promise I will be careful." She watched Peter leave in the rearview mirror. Confident he was out of earshot she leaned forward and murmured to the car. "I know how to treat a beautiful lady, and you...you are beautiful, and you are going to purr in my hands."

"Nice car," a female voice remarked.

Maddie jumped at the voice. "What?...hey," she smiled at the woman, feeling her cheeks redden as she prayed that her one-sided conversation with the car hadn't been heard. She got out of the car and stood beside it. "It's a loaner while my car is in the shop. I don't think we've met?" she said holding her hand out. "Maddie Marinelli."

Smiling, Teddy took her hand and shook it. "I have heard a *lot* about you, Doctor Marinelli...Claudia Roosevelt."

Maddie tried to think where she had heard the name before. Teddy watched the slight twitch of Maddie's eye as she wracked her brain. "You've probably heard me called Teddy, I'm the manhole aunt," Teddy said helpfully.

"Of course," Maddie exclaimed. "I thought I'd heard your name before but couldn't place it."

"Yeah, well I got in trouble with the whole manhole thing." Teddy winced. "Anyway, I have a date with my shower, and then I'm going to curl up and let the hangover, that's about a couple of hours off appearing, destroy my Saturday."

Maddie gave a soft laugh. "Big night?"

"Tequila with Alex. It seemed like a really good idea, right up until I woke up on the porch swing this mornin'." Teddy watched

Maddie's reaction carefully when she mentioned her friend and had to hide a smirk as she saw something light up on Maddie's face at Alex's name. "Nice to meet you, Doc," she said, starting to trudge towards her home.

"Good to meet you too," Maddie said, twirling the car key around her finger. She paused for a moment then turned back and into the house.

Teddy walked slowly, feeling like her body and mind were treading through treacle, she dug around in her pocket and brought out her phone. "Make you purr huh." She chuckled as she squinted at her cell trying to focus on the screen while willing her clumsy fingers to type a text. She grinned at the content which simply said 'You're gonna lose' before pressing the send button.

Ruth was bustling around the kitchen when the sound of a text arriving on her phone interrupted her activities. She laughed at the words on her screen before typing her response, 'This would be one bet I wouldn't mind losing' pocketing her phone, she shook her head and giggled to herself.

Maddie entered the coffee shop, humming softly to herself. She had driven Peter's T-Bird less than a mile.

But what a ride.

She decided that since there was no clinic today, she would take the opportunity to go for a drive. However, breakfast was a priority and, since she had nothing in, she had opted to pay a visit to Ruby's. She had told herself that it was just for that reason and not because she hoped to see Alex.

"Morning, Doc," Lou greeted. "Is that Peter's car?" she asked spotting the red Thunderbird through the window.

"Yes, it is, and we're heading out for a drive together, just as soon as I get a coffee and something to eat." Maddie smiled, handing Lou the travel mug that Alex had given her.

Lou looked surprised. The T-Bird was Peter's pride and joy. She wasn't even allowed to sit in her brother-in-law's car and here he was lending it to a virtual stranger who, apparently, was about to drink coffee in it. She started to pour coffee into the mug. "So where you thinking of heading?" Lou asked as she added milk to the cup.

"I'm not sure. Do you have any recommendations?" Maddie asked, looking absently at the pastries in the display cabinet.

"The road out to the Falls is lovely," Lou mused, pushing the lid onto the mug and walking back towards Maddie. "Or you could head out west, that's quite a nice drive." She paused as she remembered a task that Alex was due to complete that day. She clicked her fingers. "Actually, if you take the Falls road, could you do me a favor, and drop something off?" She scurried off into the kitchen, returning a moment later with a full container box. "This is a delivery for Glenda Hayes, she lives out that way. Alex was going to deliver it today but, judging from the phone call I got from her earlier, she's probably not in a fit state to drive."

"Yeah I met Teddy earlier, and she said they'd had a bit of a night." Maddie laughed. "So where is this place?"

Lou picked up a napkin and spent the next five minutes drawing a map to the Hayes' home and giving Maddie instructions. Finally, sure that she had a good idea where she was going, Maddie picked up the box and the napkin and headed out to the car.

She took a sip of coffee as she drove following Lou's neatly drawn map. It was only when her stomach rumbled that she realized that she had forgotten, thanks to all the 'directions' chatter, to get something to eat. Her eyes trailed lazily down to the container sitting on top of her grey hooded top on the passenger seat beside her. She chewed nervously on her lip feeling the draw of the contents pull her in. Eventually, her hunger dictated the decision. She nestled her coffee mug between her thighs and pried the lid from the container, glancing down greedily at the brownies that were packed into the box.

"Sorry Mrs. Hayes," she muttered lifting a brownie and sighing in pleasure as she took her first bite. She quickly finished it licking her fingers to make sure that she didn't waste a crumb of the delicious treat. A minute later her hand inched back towards the box to snag another brownie. "Just this one I promise," she said, taking a hungry bite.

∞ ∞ ∞

Alex groaned loudly. "Why are you shouting?" she asked in a pained tone.

"I'm not!" Lou said defensively. "It's not my fault that you and Teddy got as drunk as a three-eyed spider on a blue tick dog last night," she added, crossing her arms disapprovingly.

Alex bent over and thumped her head down onto the counter. "Kill me. Just put me out of my misery." She picked up the large knife sitting on the chopping board beside her and held it out behind her towards Lou.

"Don't tempt me," Lou replied. She turned to leave then, remembering the day's earlier events, spun back around. "Oh you don't need to thank me by the way, but I've saved you a drive out to the Hayes' today. The doc's taking the delivery out."

Alex snapped upright, wavering slightly at the head rush the action caused.

"What did you say?"

"The doc, she came in for breakfast and was going out for a drive, so I suggested the Falls road, and if she was going that way she could drop off Mrs. Hayes' delivery. Oh God, I just realized, we got so distracted about the drive, she didn't order any food." Lou shrugged.

Her eyes widened as Alex walked towards her with the large knife still in her hand. "When did Madeleine come in here?"

"'bout four hours ago?" Lou replied, not sure why Alex was suddenly acting so anxiously and pointing the kitchen knife in her direction.

"She was driving out to the Falls in the golf cart?"

Lou shook her head. "Nope! That would be ridiculous! Peter's given her his T-Bird. Which I think is odd 'cause...are you listening to me?" Lou asked as Alex picked up the phone, tapping the side of the knife against her leg nervously as she waited for whoever she was calling to answer.

"Hey, Glenda...Hi, it's Alex...I'm great thanks...I just wondered have you seen the new doc?" She paused as she listened to the response. "No...oh!" Her eyes narrowed as she shot Lou a glare. "Okay. Well, I just wanted you to know that I may struggle to get out to you today. Would Monday be okay? Do you have enough?" She nodded as she listened, though she was eager to end the call. "Okay, I'll see you Monday. Take care," she said, smiling into the phone.

The same smile immediately disappeared as she slammed the phone down. "No...no...no...no...no...no...no," she muttered running a hand through her hair as she pointed the tip of the knife towards Lou. "Do you have any idea what you could have done?"

Lou looked at Alex in puzzlement. "I have *no* idea what you're talking about."

Alex put the knife down with a loud clatter and started to pace, mumbling to herself.

"She should have been there unless she maybe goes in on her way back...that would be a possibility...but if she hasn't and if she's...Oh God," she groaned, grabbing her car keys.

"What?" Lou asked still none the wiser as to what her boss what going on about.

"The delivery for Glenda is...special," Alex said slowly. "I make her *special* brownies to help with her MS."

Lou's mouth gaped open. "Those were pot cakes!" she almost yelled.

Alex shushed her. "Do you want the whole town to know!" She pushed open the door of the kitchen and lifted the counter. "I'm going to go see if I can spot her. You're now on your own today and if Matt comes in tell him to keep Jessica until I call him."

∞ ∞ ∞

Tapping her fingers impatiently against the steering wheel, Alex drove the empty Falls road. She scanned the distance for a glimpse of the red of Peter's T-Bird and let out a relieved sigh when she spotted it parked at a jaunty angle beside the road. She pulled her car up behind the stationary vehicle, got out and looked in through the window. Her shoulders slumped as she realized the car was empty before her face crumpled into a tearless sob of dismay when she spotted the plastic container, now only housing a few stray crumbs.

"Oh God, she's eaten the lot."

She turned shielding her eyes from the sun and swept her head from side to side trying to spot the doctor. "Madeleine!" she shouted, groaning as she received no response. She shouted several more times, eventually hearing a distant 'Alex, is that you?' in reply. She almost jumped into the air at the sound and sped off in the direction of the shout. "Where are you?" she shouted.

"Alex, you have got to see this!" Maddie yelled.

Alex ran to where she spotted a flash of grey against the brush and trees, then skidded to a halt as she saw Maddie bending over and pointing towards something on the ground. Her eyes widened in horror as she finally saw what Maddie was pointing at.

"Be vewy, vewy, quiet," Maddie said, mimicking Elmer Fudd with her finger placed haphazardly against her lips. "This is my friend Pepe," Maddie said with a large messy grin on her face. "Pepe, meet Alex."

About three feet from Maddie, watching her movements carefully, was one of the biggest skunks that Alex had ever seen.

"Madeleine, I need you to come to me...real slowly," Alex said gulping.

Maddie looked at Alex. "You look pretty."

Alex couldn't help the smile that tugged at her lips.

"Well thank you, Madeleine, but right now I really need you to come over here by me."

"No, not pretty." Maddie's face scrunched up, and she shook her head. Alex's eyebrows rose at the rescinded compliment. "Hot, I mean *really* hot," Maddie said nodding. "Like rip your clothes off and kiss you all over hot."

Alex swallowed hard at that thought. "Okay, Madeleine. I'm *super* flattered, but really right now I need you here."

"You do?" Maddie replied sexily. "That's good 'cause I really want to do things to you...naughty things," she purred. She slowly stood up straight and started to walk towards Alex, who was torn between breathing a sigh of relief and holding her breath at Maddie's proclamation.

"Oh wait." she pointed back behind her. "I need to say bye to Pepe."

She turned back quickly, ignoring the cry from Alex who could do nothing but watch in horror as the quick movement finally startled the animal. In one swift motion it planted its front legs and spun around with its tail in the air. Maddie recoiled as the spray hit her square in the chest.

"Oh God," she screamed, flapping her hands in the air.

"It's okay, you're okay," Alex said approaching her. Immediately the acrid smell from the skunk's only defense invaded her nostrils, and she started to gag. "Don't touch it," she instructed as Maddie retched. She turned away from Maddie and took a deep breath. Holding it in she quickly moved towards the tall doctor and started to pull the loose-fitting grey hooded top, carefully with her fingertips, up over Maddie's head. When she had it free, she held it at arm's length before tossing it as far as she could into the bush.

"Hey!" Maddie said, watching her top land on top of a bush.

"Trust me, you don't want that top anymore," Alex replied, leaning down to smell Maddie's T-shirt to see whether the spray had managed to get through more than the first layer of material. She managed artfully to block from her mind that she was inches from Maddie's breasts as she undertook this task. Her nose wrinkled at the smell. "Yeah, you need to lose the T-shirt too."

Maddie gave a deep chuckle. "Are you trying to get me naked?"

"Seriously, as much as I really want to get you naked, you smelling of skunk is not how I pictured it happening," Alex muttered, pulling at the hem of Maddie's T-shirt to encourage her to lift her arms. She peeled the shirt from her and tossed it in the same direction as the hoodie.

Maddie stood in her bra, with one eyebrow cocked teasingly. "You wanna smell the bra, in case that needs to go too?"

Momentarily, Alex lost the power of speech. Her mouth opened and closed as she considered the offer. She let out a quiet growl as she pulled off the hooded college top that was an integral part of her customary hangover self-pity outfit. "Put this on," she said handing it over to Maddie, who flashed a disappointed look at her.

They walked back towards the cars in silence. "Gimme the keys," Alex instructed, holding her hand out. "I'll drive you back." She decided that leaving her car out on the road would not result in Peter throwing a hissy fit that would occur if the T-Bird was abandoned.

"I..." Maddie looked at her. Her lips pursed as she tried to remember what she'd done with them.

"Please don't tell me they were in your top," Alex practically wailed.

"Umm." Maddie dug her hands into her jeans' pockets. A look of relief washed over her face as her fingers found the key for the car.

"Thank God. Right, get in." Alex opened the passenger door, and Maddie slumped into the seat pushing the empty brownie container onto the floor before she sat on it.

By the time Alex had run around the hood, Maddie was deep in concentration studying her hand. "There are twenty-seven bones in the hand," Maddie said. Her tone was awestruck as she twisted her hand back and forth. "Isn't that amazing!"

"Awesome," Alex replied absently as she put the key into the ignition. "Put your seatbelt on." Her mind was whirring with what

Maddie had said moments before the skunk struck. She knew that, in part, the amount of drugs in Maddie's system could be responsible for lowering her inhibitions. However, the thought that was persistently hammering at her head was that those feelings must have been there already. The drugs wouldn't create those. She turned to check that Maddie had her seatbelt fastened. Seeing that the doctor was still looking intently at her hand, she rolled her eyes and leaned across her to grab the other half of the lap belt.

Maddie dropped her hand as Alex's head appeared under her chin as she rummaged around to locate the seat belt. She took in a deep breath, inhaling the coconut scent from Alex's hair. "You smell way better than a skunk."

Alex snorted as she pulled the belt over Maddie's lap and fastened the latch. "You really know how to flatter a lady." She looked up into Maddie's eyes. Her smile froze in place as she saw Maddie's pupils dilate, making her brown eyes appear almost black, and focusing dangerously on her lips. "I need to get you back to town," Alex said in a ragged voice, as she pulled her body back from the warmth of Maddie's. Her heart thumped in her chest as she turned the car in the direction of town.

"I really do," Maddie snaked a hand up Alex's arm. "I can flatter for hours."

"Okay, space cadet, you need to take your twenty-seven bones, and put them on your lap," Alex huffed, trying to keep her composure.

Maddie chuckled, withdrawing her hand and putting it on her lap as instructed. They drove for a few minutes until Maddie broke the silence. "I'm really hungry, do you have any more brownies?" she asked looking down towards the empty container.

Rolling her eyes, Alex gently pulled her back into her seat. "I really think you've had enough brownies for one day."

Chapter Five

Maddie cracked one eye open. Immediately it narrowed in confusion. She had no idea where she was. She was in a comfortable bed, but not her own, and so she shifted trying to give her one open eye a better view of her surroundings.

"Hey, sleepy head."

Her other eye snapped open as she recognized the voice behind her. She slowly turned over. Sitting up on the bed next to her, and reading, was Alex.

"Hey," she responded. Her throat felt dry, and her head was fuggy.

Alex handed her a glass of water. "Drink this."

Maddie sat up, and the covers fell from her as she moved. She grabbed at them as she suddenly became conscious of her nakedness. She took the glass avoiding Alex's eyes. "What happened? Did we?"

"What do you remember?" Alex asked.

"I was driving and eating those brownies that Lou gave me, and after about a half hour I started to feel a bit weird, so I pulled over." She screwed her face up in concentration. "After that, I'm a bit hazy."

Alex closed her book and placed it on her nightstand. "You mean you don't remember?" She frowned and held her hand against her chest. "We had the most amazing sex I've ever had. I mean really amazing and you don't...Oh God, I feel so stupid."

Maddie's jaw slackened. "Oh, my God...I...we..."

"Relax, Madeleine, I'm teasing." Alex laughed. "I'm sorry. Those brownies were hash cakes. I make them for Glenda to help with the symptoms of her MS. I found you out on the road. You were higher than a sweet Georgia pine."

Maddie nodded. She was relieved that they hadn't slept together as she'd no recollection of it. That would be something she wanted to be in complete control for. "So is there a reason why I'm in your bed naked? And..."—she sniffed as her nose caught an unusual smell—"why do I smell of tomatoes?"

"You got zapped by a skunk, so I brought you back here to get cleaned up, and sleep it off. Tomato juice takes the smell away."

"What time is it?" Maddie asked.

Alex checked her watch. "Ten p.m. Can I get you anything?"

"I'm kinda hungry," Maddie admitted. "Could I have some oatmeal or something?"

Alex smiled. "Sure."

Maddie looked down under the covers. "Did you...?" She stopped, giving Alex an anxious look.

"You did that by yourself." Alex patted the covers above Maddie's thigh.

"Oh...did I do or say anything?"

Alex looked up towards the ceiling and let out a soft breath. "Do anything, no. Say anything, well let's say you were...enlightening!"

Maddie raised her eyebrows questioningly.

"There are twenty-seven bones in the hand," Alex said, leaving the room.

Maddie let out a long sigh relieved that she hadn't made a complete fool of herself.

"Oh"—Alex's head popped around the doorframe—"and that I'm hot and you want to do naughty things to me." She grinned and disappeared downstairs to fetch Maddie's oatmeal.

Her foot had only touched the first step when she heard Maddie's anguished cry from her bedroom.

Maddie pulled herself out of Alex's bed, mortified that she had apparently thrown herself at the blonde woman while off her head. She pulled on her jeans and scanned the room for the rest of her clothes. Unable to find them, she picked up a soft flannel shirt that Alex had laid beside her jeans and put it on. She tiptoed down the stairs not sure whether Jessica was in bed and, when she reached the kitchen, stood in the doorway watching as Alex hummed to herself while making her oatmeal.

Alex moved around her kitchen humming nervously as her mind worked overtime. It had been spinning ever since Maddie had announced that she wanted to do 'naughty things' with her. Now Maddie was awake and knew what she'd said, Alex felt uncertain as to what her next move would be.

She stirred the oatmeal. Satisfied with its consistency, she poured it into a bowl and collected a spoon. She almost dropped both as she turned and spotted Maddie standing in the doorway. "Oh hey," she said in surprise. "I was going to bring it up to you."

"It's okay, you've already done so much," Maddie replied, moving into the kitchen and taking a seat. "I couldn't find my clothes," she added, giving the shirt a small tug.

"Yeah, your sweat top and T-shirt are decorating a bush, and your bra is in the wash. It wasn't too bad, but there was still a slight smell coming from it." She placed the oatmeal down in front of Maddie, who eyed it nervously, unable to look at Alex without embarrassment coursing through her.

"Thank you," she said quietly, picking up the spoon. "Is Jessica here?"

"Matt's."

Maddie coughed awkwardly as Alex placed a cup of coffee in front of her and sat down, cradling the cup in her hands.

"About what I said." Her hand stirred the spoon in the oatmeal watching as the thick gloop quickly covered over the trail the spoon made.

Alex cocked her head to the side waiting for Maddie to continue.

"I'm not in the habit of propositioning women like that."

Alex brought the mug of coffee up to her lips. "I should hope not," she replied, a small smirk playing on her lips.

"I...I'm sorry," Maddie said, raising her head slightly and giving Alex a quick glance.

"Did you mean it?" Alex put her mug down and rested her arms on the table, leaning forward towards Maddie.

Maddie looked up. Her mouth opened and closed several times as she attempted to speak but, unsure of how to approach the topic, she remained silent. Her eyebrows furrowed as her brain rifled through the options. Finally, she settled on absolute honesty. "Yes." She bit her top lip. "I'm sorry though. I would have never...had I not been," she whirled her fingers around at her temple. "I'm sorry if I made you uncomfortable." She looked back down at her oatmeal. Her appetite had vanished as her stomach churned with nerves.

"It's okay," Alex replied, stretching her hand across the table and placing it on top of Maddie's. "I'm glad that you said it because I've been sensing this"—her hand twirled as she tried to find the right word—"connection." Maddie looked up at the word. "Between us."

Maddie's eyes widened slightly at Alex's admission. "You have?"

Alex nodded and smiled. "I have, Madeleine." She took a breath to prepare herself to say words that hadn't left her mouth for almost a decade. "I'm gay."

Maddie gave a soft laugh. "Snap, my marriage was to Joanna."

Smiling, Alex pulled her hand away and picked up her mug in both hands. "Ha, my vajaydar is never wrong," she said proudly.

"Your what?"

Alex waved her hand. "A Teddyism, ignore me."

Maddie picked up the coffee mug. "So this connection that you sensed...?" She left the end of her query hanging hoping that Alex would understand the rest.

Pausing for what seemed like an eternity, Alex finally spoke. "It's mutual, I want to do naughty things with you too." Her tone was sad, however, and Maddie picked up on this immediately.

"It sounds like there's a 'but' in there."

Taking a deep breath, Alex finally knew what she had to do. "You are amazing. You're gorgeous and funny and smart." She looked into Maddie's gentle eyes. "I like you...and it won't take a whole lot for me to *really* like you, but"—she smiled as she finally said the word that Maddie had been expecting—"you are going soon and I..." She shook her head sadly. "I have been on my own for so long. I mean a long time and I really miss sex. But your bringing me coffee the other day made me realize that I'd forgotten what that was like and it made me want to not be alone anymore, and then to see you sleeping in my bed today." She paused as she reflected on the emotions she had experienced. "I sat there because I've forgotten what it felt like to have someone other than Jessica lying beside me. I'm sorry." She huffed. "I used to be okay at no strings."

"Are you saying you care enough about me not to sleep with me?" Maddie gave her a soft smile. She immediately understood the turmoil that Alex was going through. She was sure that were they to do what she wanted, saying goodbye and leaving would become more difficult for both of them.

"Guess I'm more like Matt than I thought." Alex forced a laugh. The falseness of it caught her throat. "Who knew." She blinked as tears pricked her eyes. She felt foolish at their appearance and stood up to hide them from Maddie. She stood at the sink and puffed up her cheeks releasing a slow breath. Her vision became blurred from the tears still pooling in her eyes.

Maddie got up and walked over to her pulling the smaller woman into an embrace. "If you ever decide that you don't like me, then I will be right here."

Alex laughed and sniffed, resting her chin on Maddie's shoulder. "Oh don't worry, you will be the first to know!"

∞ ∞ ∞

They drove in silence in the dark. Maddie had insisted on taking Alex out to collect her car from the Falls road. For the most part of the journey, their conversation had settled back into the flirty banter that they had exchanged before their heart-to-heart in Alex's kitchen. However, now both were lost in their thoughts. Maddie allowed her eyes to leave the road as she glanced over towards Alex.

"So how long is long?" she asked.

Alex shook her head slightly as Maddie's voice roused her from her thoughts. "For what?...Oh, that!" She gave a chuckle as she realized what Maddie was asking, "Loooong. Since before Jessica."

Maddie's head spun around, and the action made her swerve erratically on the empty road.

"That's...wow...seriously! But she's what, six?"

"Seven and believe me, it's not something I want to brag about," Alex said out of the side of her mouth. "I did go on a couple dates a while back, but we didn't connect in that way. So, yup, for years it's just been me and the rabbit."

"Buttercup?" Maddie asked confused.

Alex furrowed her brow. "What? No! Not that kind of rabbit! I haven't reached the realms of bestiality." She laughed.

"Oh...Ohh!" Maddie nodded as she realized what kind of rabbit Alex was referring to. "Sorry." She looked ahead at the road. "Was it tough? I mean, it's a small town."

Alex narrowed her eyes as she tried to concentrate on the conversation leaps. "Coming out you mean? I guess. None of my friends seemed that bothered. I realized when I was in high school and then there was the whole Charlotte Grace thing on Ruth's mom's bed. I don't know if I was more angry or relieved when Matt stopped us." She picked at the hem of her jeans as she recalled being sixteen, full of hormones and confused at the feelings she was having. "He threw her out then sat on the bed and told me that it shouldn't be like that; a drunken fumble with someone who didn't love me and had their own agenda. It should be with someone I loved and who loved me. See, he's not just the manwhore that he gets painted as," she said, seeing Maddie's surprise, "and when I had the support of my friends and family the rest of the town didn't really matter. We caused more outrage getting pregnant the way we did, but that was all forgotten when Jessica was born early. The whole town sent us messages of support." She spotted her car where she had left it earlier in the day. "There it is." She pointed, while feeling sad that they had reached their destination and her time with Maddie would be at an end.

Maddie pulled the Thunderbird to a halt behind Alex's car and put the handbrake on. She left the engine running so that the headlights bathed the vehicle in light.

"Thank you for bringing me out," Alex said, giving her a grateful smile. She opened the door and walked towards her car. As she unlocked the driver's door, she heard a door slam behind her and the sound of footsteps on the gravel. She turned and saw a slightly flushed and out of breath Maddie in front of her.

"Wha—" She never completed the word as Maddie took her cheeks in her hands and pressed her lips against hers. Immediately the kiss deepened as Alex's back hit the car. They kissed each other with a sense of desperation, as their hands pulled at each other to increase their contact. Alex swept her tongue between Maddie's lips, moaning as the taller woman parted them to allow her access. They instinctively created a dance with their mouths, each woman taking control before allowing the other to dictate the pace and strength of the kiss. Finally, panting, they pulled apart, their lips still inches from each other.

"I'm sorry, but I couldn't not know what that would feel like," Maddie whispered, swallowing hard at the lump that had appeared in her throat.

"It's okay," Alex said in response, leaning forward and placing a delicate kiss on Maddie's lips.

Pulling back Maddie gave Alex a soft smile. "I don't want to sleep with you either."

She walked back towards her car leaving Alex smiling at her roundabout way of telling her that she cared about her.

Chapter Six

"Hi, I'm sorry we're late," Alex apologized, shouting from Ruth's hallway. She stripped off hers and Jessica's jackets, then picked up the box with dessert in it and headed towards the dining room. "Someone couldn't decide what shade of pink to wear, and by someone, I don't mean me..." She stopped as she entered the room, immediately spotting Maddie sitting at the table next to Sully. "Hi," she said breathlessly, her eyes fixed on Maddie.

"Hi," Maddie replied, a shy smile on her lips.

The rest of the room looked at each other, feeling the tension between the two women.

"And my girl looks very pretty in pink," Sully announced in order to break the silence that had developed.

"Maddie-Lyn," Jessica cried running around the table, past her father's outstretched arms and threw herself into the doctor's lap.

"Hello, Daddy, I love you, Daddy," Sully muttered in a joking tone. "You're now like chopped liver to me, Daddy."

Jessica leaned over and planted a wet kiss on his cheek. "Silly, Daddy, I see you all the time," she scolded her pouting father.

Alex handed the box to Ruth. "Sorry I didn't have time to make the usual," she apologized taking her seat next to Teddy.

"No worries." Ruth grinned, before taking the box into the kitchen, holding a hand to her stomach.

"Is that *special* dessert?" Lou asked, the sides of her mouth quirking into a smile as she looked over at Maddie who blushed and concentrated on Jessica.

Scowling over at her assistant, Alex gave an almost imperceptible shake of her head. "All my baking is special...Louise," she said pointedly.

Sully looked at the two women. "She full-named you. What did you just do?"

All attention was now on Lou who shrunk in her seat. "Nothing, not important." She shrugged. "I'm going to go help Ruth with the food." She stood up and scuttled off into the kitchen.

Teddy watched Alex carefully as she surreptitiously kept an eye on Maddie whose attention was focused on the young girl sitting on her lap. She leaned over and whispered in Alex's ear. "Your vajaydar was right, wasn't it."

Alex slowly turned her head to glare at her friend. "We are not going to have this conversation, not here," she whispered in return.

"What's with the whispering?" Sully complained, feeling left out.

"I was just saying that I thought you were starting to look old," Teddy lied smoothly. "Alex here said you looked distinguished."

Before Sully could respond Ruth, Lou and Peter entered the room with the meal. Peter placed the roast grandly in the center of the table, as his wife and sister-in-law put the vegetables down.

"Welcome, Maddie to our regular Sunday insult session," Ruth said, gripping Teddy's shoulders as she passed on her way to her seat.

Teddy held up her wine glass. "Welcome and, to be fair, it's usually only Sully that we insult."

"You insult," Alex added. "Jessica, let Madeleine eat," she said, pushing out the seat next to her to encourage her daughter around. The girl grumbled but slipped off Maddie's lap and crawled under the table to get to her seat.

"So, Ruth, how are you keeping?" Maddie asked.

"Good, I've been getting some cramps the past couple of days though." She frowned.

"Probably just Braxton-Hicks," Maddie said, passing the potatoes on.

"Pretty sure I've got her CD," Sully said grinning.

Maddie laughed, before returning her attention to Ruth. "If you want, you can come into the surgery, and I can check you over."

"Yeah, I'll come in tomorrow," Ruth replied. "It's good to have a doc back in town again." She smiled.

As they ate dinner, the conversation flowed easily between the old friends and their new guest. Ruth and Teddy exchanged questioning glances as they caught the odd look between Maddie and Alex during the meal.

"So, Maddie are you going to come with us to the bar afterwards?" Ruth asked. "We usually head down there for a couple of drinks and a game of pool."

Before answering, Maddie looked at Alex. "I'd love to," she replied when Alex gave her a half smile.

"I'll go get dessert," Alex said, collecting their empty plates and disappearing into the kitchen. She had only just escaped into the kitchen when she was quickly joined by Teddy.

"Okay, Milne, spill."

Sighing, Alex placed the chocolate muffins she had brought onto plates. "There's nothing to spill."

"Like shit there's not," Teddy replied, helping to dish out the muffins.

Alex stopped and looked at her friend. "The vajaydar was right, and she's attracted to me." She turned her attention back to the food.

"You're not going to do anything about it though are you." Teddy sighed.

"No, I'm not," Alex said sadly. "I like her, and I could really fall for her, and that scares me because then I would have to say goodbye."

Teddy rubbed her shoulder. "Better to love and lose than not love at all."

Alex looked deep into her friend's eyes. "That's bullshit, and you know it, Teddy. You're no different to me. You haven't had a relationship that's lasted more than two weeks since Bear died. You're terrified of loving and losing so don't lecture me." She bit her lip with regret at how harsh her words had come out. "I'm sorry."

Teddy pulled her into a hug. "No, you're right. I am full of shit. You do what's best for you, I'll always have your back. Although you do realize that you're losing me money."

"You bet on me with Ruth didn't you?" Alex said laughing and still hugging her friend.

"As soon as Ruth said she was asking questions about you," Teddy confirmed, releasing her friend and picking up the dessert plates. Alex shook her head and followed Teddy back to the dining room.

∞ ∞ ∞

The evening caught up with them quickly as they laughed and played each other at pool in Sullivan's Bar. Not sure if she was now verging on self-harm territory, Maddie took every opportunity for any physical contact with Alex. While her head understood the reasons for them not taking their feelings further, her body was crying out to touch, and be touched.

Teddy watched, sitting beside Ruth as the two women played a flirtatious game of pool.

"They look good together," Ruth mused. "You sure that they're not..."

Shaking her head, Teddy took a drink from her beer bottle. "Nope, Alex doesn't want it to be a passing through thing. Although I think that given half a chance and a change in circumstance they would be at it on that table."

"Now that would be something I would pay for," Sam said, sitting down at the table behind them.

"Sam Hunter, you and your filthy little mind," Ruth admonished with a half laugh. "I'm of a mind to tell your big sister on you. I'm sure Erin would have something to say about your remark."

The mechanic gave a lazy shrug. "Pretty sure Erin would go halves with me. Besides, it's my filthy little mind that got you the doctor here in case you ever decide to have that child you've been lugging around for, what's it been...like a year?"

Ruth's eyes narrowed. "What do you mean?" She had suspected that her husband and Sam had been up to something but couldn't get to the bottom of it. "Sam, what do you mean?" she pressed.

"I mean that you don't need to thank me, but it was my idea not to give her the parts for the car until you give birth."

Ruth's mouth gaped open. "You have the parts for her car?" she asked quietly.

Sam nodded. "Have since she arrived." He squeaked as Ruth grabbed him by the collar and dragged him up to the bar where Peter was talking to Sully.

"Tell me you haven't," she hissed.

Peter looked at his wife in confusion. "Haven't what?"

She pulled Sam around so that he was standing next to him. "Tell me you haven't listened to this halfwit and kept Maddie here when she didn't need to be."

Sam looked over towards the pool table where the tall doctor and Alex were still playing their game. "She's hardly a hostage," he scoffed.

"You. Are not allowed to speak," Ruth snarled, turning back to her husband. "Him, I expect this sort of thing from," she said pointing at Sam. "He got hit around the head a lot at school...but you!" She shook her head in disappointment. "What about you? Did you know?" She turned on Sully who was standing behind the bar.

Sully held his hands up. "Just hearing it for the first time. Although I can't say I blame him. Jessica's only here because this town had a doc and nurse in it," he admitted.

Ruth looked at the three men. "Fix her car. You hear me, Peter Campbell? You will fix her car first thing tomorrow and let that woman get on her way. I can't believe you two." She rolled her eyes. "Oh for God's sake, Sam, will you be careful," she half-bellowed.

"Whaaaat?" Sam wailed, unsure what he was in more trouble about.

"Your damn drink, you just poured it on my foot."

Sam held up his full bottle of beer. "Haven't spilled a drop." He looked at her, his face scrunched in confusion.

Looking down at her feet Ruth's shoulders slumped. "Oh crap," she muttered. "My waters have broken."

∞ ∞ ∞

"Okay, so everything sounds fine, you're not in labor yet, so we wait twenty-four hours, and if nothing happens, then we induce." Maddie wound her stethoscope back around her neck. "Get comfy, we could be here for a while." She pulled Ruth's top down and covered her up with the blanket.

Peter stood beside his wife's hospital bed. "Isn't it dangerous for the baby?" he asked, his face creased with worry.

Maddie gave him an encouraging smile. "The risk is only slight unless you were planning on having sex?" she asked with one eyebrow raised.

Peter looked expectantly at his wife.

"Not a hope in hell, Peter Campbell," Ruth replied, nudging him with her shoulder.

Laughing, Maddie gave Ruth a pat on the arm. "I'll just go let everyone know that they can shoot off. You stay relaxed."

"I am," Ruth said cheerily.

Maddie called over her shoulder as she opened the door. "I was talking to Peter!"

The group of friends stood up from their various positions around the waiting room. Sully was cradling a sleeping Jessica in his arms. Maddie held her hands up. "You might as well all go home. Her waters have broken, but there's no sign of labor pains yet, so it's going to be a long night."

Sully shifted Jessica on his shoulder. "Okay, well this one needs her bed. Alex, you taking her home or will I?" he asked looking over the top of Jessica's head towards her mother.

"I'll take her." Alex smiled as Sully started to walk out. "But you're carrying her to mine," she added following him towards the door. Her hands were clasped in front of her as if she were holding them close to stop her from reaching out. "Have a good night Madeleine," she said quietly. She cocked her head to the side and looked as though she was going to say more before giving a smile then flicking her hair from her face.

Maddie felt her body move forward as Alex turned to leave. It was as if she were being pulled by a powerful undertow; a force connecting her to Alex. When there was a change in the physical distance between them, she was unable to stop herself from trying to reduce it.

"Okay, everyone enjoy your sleep," Maddie said, ushering them out of the clinic. She was standing watching their departure with her head leaning on her hand, which was pressed against the wooden doorframe when a door opened in the clinic behind her.

"Sam!" Peter's head appeared around the examination room door.

Sam turned with an expectant look and climbed the stairs to look back into the clinic.

"Ruth says tonight. Fix it, tonight." His head disappeared before Sam could respond.

"Looks like I won't be getting any sleep," the mechanic grumbled to himself shaking his head as he hopped back down the steps.

Alex paused at the end of the pathway, moving out of the way as Sam brushed past her. She brought her hand up into a small wave before setting off in pursuit of Sully.

"Night," Maddie called, then closed the clinic door and checked her watch. "Nine o' clock," she said aloud. "And I'm going to need my body weight in coffee," she murmured heading off towards the small kitchen area.

∞ ∞ ∞

"Is there a reason I'm only now finding out that we have a baby coming?"

Maddie looked up from the paperwork she was completing, towards the doorway of the office. Mack was standing with her hands on her hips regarding Maddie with one of her infamous stares. Maddie sighed, put her pen down and ran her hands through her hair. Her eyes closed in pleasure as she scraped her nails against her scalp.

"Mack, it's"—she checked the clock—"eleven p.m. She's not in labor, we're waiting it out." She blinked to focus her tired eyes on her nurse. "You can go home, I've got it."

"Ummm-hmmm," Mack said, walking into the room. "When was the last time you helped a woman give birth?"

Maddie closed her eyes and took in a deep breath. "She's in exam room one, you take the bed in room two, and I'll stay here," she replied, her voice tinged with resignation.

"Knew you'd see it my way." Mack chuckled as she headed out of the room in a cocky waddle.

Picking up her pen Maddie scowled. "I'm not afraid of her, I am not afraid of her," she chanted under her breath. "Much." She chuckled inwardly with a shake of her head.

∞ ∞ ∞

Maddie peeked around the doorway into the exam room. Ruth was lying awake, her hands resting on her swollen stomach. Soft snores were coming from Peter who was lying at an impossible angle on one of the seats. Maddie smiled at the pregnant woman and came quietly into the room. "He's going wake up sore from that," she whispered, nodding towards the sleeping man.

"Yeah, well, he deserves it. He put this lazy ass baby in here," Ruth muttered, glaring over towards her husband. "What time is it?"

"Two o'clock." Smiling, Maddie took her temperature. "All still normal, no sign of fever or anything. Baby still moving?" she asked quietly.

Ruth nodded. "Yeah and I'm getting this tightness in my stomach." She grimaced as the sensation came again.

Maddie raised her eyebrows. "How often?" she asked.

"I'm not sure maybe every half hour," Ruth replied, trying to guess how long it was since the last time.

"Okay, looks like your labor is starting." She moved around to the base of the bed and pulled a stool over to sit on while she examined her. "Let's just have a quick look." She positioned Ruth's feet into the stirrups and pulled on gloves.

"Do you like her?" Ruth asked.

Maddie looked up from her position between Ruth's legs. "Like who?"

"Alex. You've been spending time together, and I just wondered..."

After taking Ruth's legs back down and pulling the covers over her, Maddie stood up and stripped the gloves off. "Everything looks fine, and we're not going to have that conversation." She gave a terse smile and left the room.

The door clicked behind her, and she let her back press against it. She sighed as she tried to process her feelings for Alex. She wanted to respect Alex's wishes. However, the attraction that she felt for her was stronger than anything she had experienced before and Maddie knew it went beyond being just a physical attraction.

"I'd say that was a yes," Peter muttered from his seat, opening one eye to look at his wife.

∞ ∞ ∞

Maddie stretched her back. "What have we got on in the clinic today?" she asked Mack as they shared a bag of potato chips.

"Nothing that can't be moved," the nurse replied, holding up a chip and looking at it thoughtfully. "Have you ever noticed that things taste different in the middle of the night?"

"How often do you eat potato chips at three in the morning?" Maddie asked, crunching a chip in her mouth.

Mack laughed. "Not often thankfully."

They heard a loud yell coming from the exam room, and both women abandoned their snack before running at full speed along the corridor. They burst into the room where Ruth was screaming as her labor pains finally took a full grip of her body. Peter looked at them wide-eyed as his wife transformed from a mild-mannered woman into a beast from another world. They grabbed gloves and settled down to work.

"Okay, Ruth, I need you to breathe for me." Maddie smiled. "Mack there has the gas and air and, if you're lucky, she might give you a hit of it."

Holding the mask up, Mack smiled. "Only if you do what you're told though."

Ruth looked at them, then released the breath that she had been holding since the wave of agony had hit her. It had been unlike any of the previous pains she'd had. The air blasted out from her mouth.

"Okay it's usually about another six hours or so from here," Maddie said, giving Ruth an apologetic smile as the woman's face fell at the news. "Hopefully we're going for a sprint finish with this little one though." Maddie smiled looking up at Mack. "Six centimeters," she said towards the nurse, receiving a nod in reply.

"Ruth, you need to relax at the top of the contractions, breathe like your jogging."

Peter snorted at the instruction. "Sorry," he said noticing the unimpressed look from the three women. "I've just never seen Ruth jog...ever."

"You want me to hit him for you?" Mack said in a flat tone.

Ruth started to laugh, the action turning into a grimace as another contraction took hold.

"Peter, now's the time for you to tell your wife how much you love her and remind her to breathe," Maddie said.

Peter nodded and gripped Ruth's hand placing his lips against the side of her damp forehead.

"I love you so much," he whispered.

Maddie and Mack exchanged a quick smile then focused on their work.

∞ ∞ ∞

At seven a.m. any tiredness that Maddie felt was quickly swept away as the first glimpse of the head of Ruth and Peter's baby appeared. "We're almost crowning," Maddie said watching intently as Ruth's body adjusted to the baby's new position.

"I need you to listen very carefully to me Ruth," Mack instructed. "You have to fight the urge to push just now, pant with me." The nurse started to pant loudly urging Ruth with her eyes to follow suit. "Seriously you're not gonna want the consequences of you pushing right now." She continued to pant, gripping Ruth's hand as the woman fought against her body's desire.

"Okay you can push now," Maddie said, looking up with a broad smile on her face. She looked back down as the baby started to emerge and swept around the baby's face to clear its airways before checking that the umbilical cord hadn't become wrapped around its neck.

The baby turned as Ruth groaned into another push, its shoulders popped out, followed quickly by the rest of its body.

"It's a boy," Maddie announced, lifting the baby up so that his parents could see him.

She handed the boy over to his crying mother's waiting arms and indicated to Mack that she should help Peter cut the cord while she finished with Ruth.

Once the cord was cut and Ruth had finished the delivery, Maddie lifted the baby from her and took him across the room to get him cleaned up. As she wrapped him in a blanket, she felt the emotion lay thick in her throat. "These hands were the first to touch you in this world little one, and they will be the first to smack you back in line," she murmured, unaware of Mack standing beside her until she heard the other woman laugh.

"I haven't heard that line for a looong time," Mack said smiling, as she thought about Alex's grandmother. "You did a great job Doc." She gave Maddie a pat on the shoulder and headed out to see what she could do about freeing up some time from the clinic to give them both a much-deserved rest.

Chapter Seven

At five p.m. a weary Maddie flopped down onto the sofa and kicked her shoes off. She and Mack had ended up running a full clinic during the day, and now exhaustion was hitting her with all its force. She groaned as her cell phone rang. Grimacing as she stood up to retrieve it, her mood lightened when she saw the photo of Zoe's face appear on the screen.

"Hey you," she said, walking back to the sofa and flopping down.

"Hey you too," Zoe replied. A smile was evident in her voice. "You sound beat."

"I am, a long labor followed by a day's clinic." Maddie rubbed the heel of her hand against her eye and yawned loudly.

"Labor? Clinic?" Zoe asked bemusedly. "What the hell are you talking about?"

"Oh God, it's been a mad couple of days. They don't have a doctor here; their last one took early retirement. So I agreed to provide some medical cover while my car is getting fixed."

"Who the hell do they think you are...Michael J. Fox?" Zoe snorted. "How the hell did you get yourself involved, Maddie?"

"I wasn't going to, then Alex came to the door with Jessica and she was having an asthma attack, and Alex looked so helpless. I couldn't say no." Maddie shuddered as she recalled the events. "You would have helped too had you been here." She shivered again for a different reason when she remembered Alex in the sweltering bathroom.

"I hope he thanked you."

"Who?"

"Alex."

Maddie let out a soft chuckle. "Alex is all woman." She could almost hear Zoe's brain working down the phone line.

"Ahhh, and there we have it. Is she cute?"

"Mmm, hadn't noticed," Maddie replied smirking.

Zoe laughed loudly. "You are so full of shit. Is she gay?"

"As a pride march in Provincetown. Oh God, Zo, she is amazing. She's gorgeous, funny, kind. Her kid is adorable. She has a lovely smile. And boy can she can kiss."

"What's the catch? Other than she's living in bumfuck nowhere."

"She doesn't want a hump and dump, and I'm just drifting through."

"What do you want?"

Maddie sat quietly for a moment. Her mind flashing through memories of her time with Alex. "To keep feeling the way I do when I'm around her."

"Oh, sweetie." Zoe sighed. "I'm happy that you're finally letting yourself feel again, but this can't end well. Like you said you're just drifting through. That little fragile heart of yours needs to be protected."

"I know," Maddie said miserably. "This sucks ass."

Zoe laughed. "Yes, it does. Now you go get some sleep. You sound like crap."

"Thanks, Mom." Maddie laughed.

"Love you, let me know when your car is fixed."

"Will do, love you too."

Maddie thumped her head against the sofa after hanging up the call. She bemoaned both her bad luck at meeting someone who had slipped past all of her defenses and not being able to pursue it. There was a knock at the door, and she contemplated getting up for it before sinking back into the sofa and yelling to whoever was there to come in. She heard the door open, soft footsteps in the hall and suddenly she was looking at the source of her disquiet.

"Hey." Alex smiled looking at the tired woman sprawled on the sofa. "I'm sorry to interrupt. I brought you some food."

Maddie flashed a grateful smile and willed her body to move from its prone position. "Thank you."

"Did you sleep at all?" Alex asked, concern apparent in her tone.

Shaking her head Maddie slowly rose from the sofa. "Not much." She took the container from Alex and started to walk into the kitchen. "Thank you for this." She brought the box up to her nose and inhaled deeply, her nose filling with the smell of the pasta dish. "Have you eaten?" she asked, moving around the kitchen looking for a plate.

Alex bit her lip, she could see how tired Maddie was, but she couldn't bring herself to leave. "Not yet."

"Wanna share?" Maddie grinned, holding the box up as if she was in a commercial.

"I'd love that." She moved to collect cutlery and carried it behind Maddie as they walked to the table. "So they're calling him Ben."

"I heard." Maddie smiled. "He's beautiful. You manage to see him?" she asked, passing Alex a plate.

Alex nodded taking the plate. "I did. I popped in earlier. You were with a patient."

Maddie nodded an acknowledgment while taking a mouthful of pasta and moaning. "This is just what the doctor ordered," she said, pointing towards the plate with her fork.

They ate in silence each stealing quick glances at the other as they did. All too soon despite their best efforts to prolong the meal, their mutual hunger meant that the food was finished. Maddie picked up the cleared plates, placing them in the dishwasher.

"That was...Heaven," she said, closing the dishwasher.

"It was only pasta." Alex shrugged.

"It was the thought that I was talking about."

Alex gave a soft laugh, she looked into Maddie's eyes which looked weighted with the lack of sleep. "Well, I should let you get some sleep." She paused beside the back door as her mind replayed the kiss they had shared. Her heart was beating so hard in her chest that she was sure that Maddie could hear it as she opened the door. Its journey was halted as Maddie placed a hand against it.

"I'm tired."

Alex looked around. "I know, you had a long night."

Maddie shook her head. "No, I'm tired of pretending that I don't want to feel you, kiss you, and now I know that you feel the same. I can't..." She held onto the door preventing it from opening further.

"We said—"

"I know," Maddie interrupted. "But I can't stop, Alex." She dropped her head and started to pepper Alex's neck with kisses. The smaller woman tipped her head back. Her eyes closed as she allowed herself to drown in the sensation of Maddie's lips on her skin.

"Please...don't," Alex said, pushing Maddie away. She looked into the brown eyes that were still heavy with tiredness but now also arousal. She swallowed hard and closed the door. The noise of the latch sounded impossibly loud in a kitchen where only the fast breaths coming from the two women overshadowed the sound of a distant ticking clock.

Alex looked down at Maddie's hand resting at her side. She threaded her fingers through the taller woman's and, licking her lips, let her gaze travel up Maddie's arm until her vision was once again fixed on brown eyes. "Not here." She moved around Maddie's body tugging gently on the hand she held and led her through the kitchen into the hall. She hesitated before starting to climb the stairs slowly.

Maddie following as Alex led them towards the bedroom. She closed the bedroom door behind them as Alex kicked off her shoes, dropping in height as she walked towards the bed in her bare feet.

She perched on the edge of the bed, placed her hands either side of her and watched as Maddie approached.

Maddie smiled. "I'm not going to have Sully burst in here and haul me off you am I?"

Alex laughed and reached out to grip the hem of Maddie's T-shirt. She pulled her closer, with Maddie stumbling slightly at the action. "God I hope not, 'cause then Jessica would have to see her mama kick her daddy's ass several shades." She wrapped her arms around Maddie and looked up. "I'll take tonight. If that's all I have you for, then I'll take it."

Her resolve not to sleep with Maddie had weakened the moment that they had kissed and even if her life had depended on it, she still could not have stopped herself.

She pushed Maddie's T-shirt up and kissed the soft olive skin of her stomach. Maddie reached down and in one swift movement, removed her shirt before allowing it to fall to the floor. She pushed gently on Alex's shoulders, pressing her down onto the mattress. Covering her body with her own, she brought their lips together in a slow sensual kiss.

Pulling back to look into blue eyes, darkened with arousal, Maddie smiled as she repositioned her weight to allow her to remove Alex's top. Their eyes never left each other as Alex lifted her torso and let Maddie's strong hands slide her shirt over her head. As soon as it was removed the warmth of Maddie's skin was immediately on her. Lifting her hands, Alex pulled Maddie's face towards her and kissed her with an intensity that surprised both of them. Suddenly, languid movements took on more purpose as fingers fought to remove remaining clothes quickly. Their desperation to rid themselves of any barriers overtook their actions. Soon they had moved to the center of the bed, and Maddie held her weight on her elbows placed either side of Alex's head. As their naked bodies pressed tightly against one another their legs entwined as they kissed.

Alex pulled on Maddie's hips, urgently needing more contact as Maddie molded their bodies closer together. Their hips moved, attuned to the rhythm of their breathing, and pushed deeper against each other. The direction of their kisses became more haphazard as they fought to taste any area of skin closest to them. Their breathing increased until both women were panting. Their bodies glistened with a light sheen of sweat as their rhythm quickened.

Finally, unable to resist the pull any longer, Maddie lifted her hand and slipped it between their slick bodies. She felt her body respond to the gasp that came from Alex's mouth as her hand moved towards the other woman's heat. The muscles in Alex's stomach tensed at the light caress and her head snapped back involuntarily as Maddie's touch became more persistent. Maddie leaned closer and pressed her lips against the exposed neck. Alex's hips moved in time until her hands reached out and gripped the covers at her side. As she let out an involuntary moan, her fists clenched the material, pulling it from the bed as her body contracted. Her back arched as she paused, her mouth open in a silent cry before her body let go of the tension and collapsed back on the bed. She looked up at Maddie who was still hovered above her with a look of wonderment on her face.

"I'm sorry." Alex laughed, she was grateful for the heat already visible in her cheeks. "It's been a while," she said apologetically.

"And it's still early. We've plenty of time to catch up on that lost time." Maddie smirked, as she lowered herself down, kissing her way down Alex's body. "Best not to waste any of it."

∞ ∞ ∞

Hazy sunlight bathed the room as Alex woke slowly. Her body ached in ways that it hadn't done for years. As her brain registered the stiffness, a smile played on her lips as she recalled the cause. She could feel the warm body of the cause of the dull ache in her muscles pressed against her back. Lips nestled against her shoulder, moving slightly with each regular breath she took as she slept.

They had continued to revel in each other until the clock which, despite several attempts, Maddie had yet to locate, struck midnight. Finally, exhaustion in both women took hold, and they had fallen asleep holding on to each other. Neither was willing to admit they were scared of waking in the morning and finding the other gone.

Alex placed her hand over Maddie's, allowing her fingers to slip between the sleeping woman's digits, knitting them together. She gave a sated sigh and allowed her brain to switch off again into a lazy doze.

When she awoke again, she was aware of dark brown eyes regarding her thoughtfully. She turned and was met with a broad smile.

"Hi."

She turned in Maddie's arms. "Hi yourself, did you sleep okay?" she asked, burrowing her head under the brunette's chin and looping her leg over Maddie's.

Maddie wound her arms tightly around the smaller woman. "Like something that sleeps really soundly," she said grinning. "You?"

"Hmm," Alex hummed in reply.

"No regrets?" Maddie asked nervously.

Alex shook her head. "None."

She felt her libido kick in again as the soft hairs leading to Maddie's sex tickled her thigh. She lifted her head and started to nibble at Maddie's neck.

"Again?" Maddie moaned playfully. "You broke me. Seriously broke me last night."

Alex lifted her head up. Her lips puckered in a pout as she flashed Maddie puppy eyes. "Really?" She moved her body so that she was on top of Maddie.

"You may actually be responsible for my death," Maddie said, her eyes wide with sincerity.

Snorting with laughter, Alex pushed herself up onto her hands and locked her elbows, taking the opportunity to push her pelvis against the woman beneath her. "But what a way to go," she replied.

Maddie moaned at the contact and flung her arms around Alex pushing the heels of her hands against her ass, kneading the soft flesh in time with Alex's movement.

"Definitely would be a happy death," Maddie agreed, craning her neck to allow her to take one of Alex's breasts into her mouth. She toyed with the nipple before releasing it with a pop. "What time is it?"

Alex looked over at the clock. "Six. We've plenty of time." She smiled, taking her bottom lip between her teeth as she watched Maddie's face flush and her brown eyes turn almost black as arousal took hold. She moved Maddie's legs so that she was positioned between them, using her own thighs to push them further apart to allow her more access.

"Time of death six o one," Maddie moaned as she hooked her legs around Alex's waist and felt her heat press directly against her own pulsing arousal. They rocked together, their breathing becoming more ragged as their passion increased. Staring into each other eyes, Alex felt the now familiar tensing of Maddie's muscles at the beginning of her orgasm. She smiled as she continued the rhythmic movements of her hips, recognizing the fluttering that signaled the start of her own climax.

Maddie lifted her torso off the bed, pulling Alex's body flush with hers. She exhaled loudly against the blonde's neck as her body released its tension. Her body twitched with aftershocks as she felt Alex ride out her own orgasm before flopping down on top of her.

"I may just have killed myself." Alex exhaled, feeling as though her heart was about to leap out of her chest it was beating so rapidly.

"How about a leisurely shower?" Maddie asked, letting her legs fall from Alex and thump softly against the bed. "Since we really smell of sex."

Alex gave a sniff against Maddie's neck. "We do. God, I've missed smelling of sex! Smelling of sex rocks!" She sat up quickly straddling Maddie's stomach. "You know what also rocks?"

Maddie cocked an eyebrow while allowing her hands to roam up Alex's thighs. "What?"

"Being first in the shower," Alex yelled, pushing her hands down onto Maddie's chest and propelling herself off the bed.

Maddie let out a loud 'Oomph' as the air was knocked out of her lungs, then set off in pursuit of a naked Alex yelling, 'Not fair,' as she ran.

∞ ∞ ∞

They stood in the bathroom with goofy grins, their eyes locked, as they dried themselves. Finally, dragging her eyes away Maddie tipped her head upside down to towel dry her hair when there was a knock at the door. She stood back up straight, stumbling slightly as the speed she generated surprised her.

"Stay here," she instructed Alex as she pulled her robe off the peg behind the door and tied it as she ran down the stairs. She opened the door to a weary-looking Sam, his blue eyes rimmed with red.

"Your car sucks ass," he moaned, holding out a set of keys. "Freaking pig of a job to do on your own."

"What?" Maddie said, taking the keys and looking at them in confusion.

Sam looked at her with a scowl. "It's fixed. It's in the shop, you can get it whenever. Just bring Peter's car in and swap." He turned and set off down the steps, before pausing and looking back, "Oh and I saw Lou on the way over. Tell Alex they're running short of Sweet'N Low." He nodded pleased that he had remembered the message.

"Okay," Maddie said absently, still looking at the keys to her car, which felt like they were burning a hole in her hand. "Wait, what do you mean tell Alex?"

"She spent the night here didn't she?" Sam replied.

Maddie's mouth opened. "How the hell!"

Holding his arms out from his side Sam shrugged. "Grace Falls!" he said as way of an explanation.

"Has no secrets," Maddie said sadly. As she swung the door shut, her attention returned to the set of keys weighing in her hand. "Or maybe just one." She tossed the keys into her medical bag at the door and turned, taking the stairs two at a time, to get back to Alex.

"Everything okay?" Alex asked as Maddie returned to the bathroom.

Maddie smiled pulling her into a hug. "Everything is wonderful."

"Who was at the door?" Alex asked, feeling her body sink into Maddie's embrace.

Placing a light kiss on Alex's exposed shoulder, Maddie closed her eyes. She hated lying, but she didn't want the reality of their situation to intrude on their time together; not when it had been so perfect. "It was Sam with a message from Lou. Apparently, the coffee shop is running short of Sweet'N Low."

Alex nodded. "Yeah I know I picked some...woah, he came here to tell me that?" she asked, as the significance of Maddie's words hit home. "Jesus, I'm beginning to think that our houses are bugged or something. How the hell?"

"That was what I said," Maddie muttered out of the side of her mouth. "Does it bother you, people knowing?" she asked, rubbing her hands up and down Alex's arms.

"No...yes...no." Alex frowned. "Does it bother you?"

Maddie shrugged. "Even if it did, I can't do anything about it, and I wouldn't swap the time with you for anything."

Alex grinned. "Oh you're smooth," she murmured against Maddie's lips.

Maddie pulled away. "And I'm all clean and freshly showered, so no getting me all worked up again," she chided.

Biting her top lip Alex reached into the shower and switched the water back on, and dropped the towel she had wound around her body.

"How about we multitask?" she pulled at the ties on Maddie's robe.

"Well, when you put it like that!" Maddie smiled allowing Alex to push the robe from her body and pull her back towards the shower. "How can I refuse?"

Chapter Eight

"C'mon, Zoe, pick up," Maddie growled tapping her fingertips impatiently against her desk as she waited for her friend to answer. The moment she heard Zoe's sleepy voice murmur 'hello,' she launched into her news. "I did it. I mean, we did it."

"What you talkin' 'bout?" Zoe yawned loudly into the phone. "Why are you calling me at the ass crack of dawn an' speaking in tongues?"

"It's not early it's..." Maddie trailed off as she remembered the time difference. "Shit, Zo, I'm sorry, it's nine here."

"It's okay, I'm assuming that by your 'we did it' you're talking about you and Alex? Although why you think I'd be interested enough in your getting some, to be woken up at seven a.m. when I'm not due in work until three, I don't know. You realize that I'll get you back when you get here."

Maddie could hear the smile in her friend's voice, and for a moment, she hesitated, as she knew that her next words would likely change her friend's expression. "About that, Zoe." Taking a deep breath, Maddie plowed on. "What would you say if I said that I was considering staying?" She closed her eyes waiting for the anticipated explosion on the other end of the line. An explosion that didn't come. "Zoe? You still there?" She heard a deep sigh. "Zo?"

"I'm here," Zoe replied. Her tone sounded exasperated. "I'm just trying to figure out what to say to you." Another few seconds passed before Maddie heard rustling then a low growl. "Okay, is it the girl, the job, or the town that's got you thinking about throwing away a perfectly good job?"

Maddie let out her breath, grateful that Zoe hadn't simply questioned her sanity and lambasted her. "All three. I can't describe this feeling, Zoe, I don't have the words to do it justice." A hesitant smile danced across her lips. The town had taken her in and appreciated what she could do to repay that kindness. Patients brought her home-made baking; although her recent experience had made her slightly wary of such produce. The office; her office, was decorated with flowers given to her by grateful patients and drawings created by kids, while she spoke to their parents, had started to adorn the walls. She had blossoming friendships and, more importantly, she had met someone who had simply taken her breath away. Her smile grew as she thought about Alex. She wasn't ready to go. She wanted to stay. She wanted to build a life in Grace Falls. Words formed in her head only to die on her lips before she put sound to them.

"I'm happy," she said finally.

"This is so unlike you, Maddie. Jesus, it took me a month of pleading with you to even consider leaving Atlanta, and you were miserable there after Joanna left."

"I know." she laughed.

Zoe must have heard something in her voice because she gave a resigned sigh. "You've become a lesbian cliché; a girl shows you her lady garden and you U-Haul your ass." She laughed. "I'm pleased for you. God knows you deserve some happiness. Just promise me that you'll take a bit more time to think this through. Speak to Alex and make sure you're both on the same page."

"You did not just call it a lady garden." Maddie snorted.

"I'm hanging up now. I'll call you later to check that you're not some imposter who has body-snatched my usually cautious friend."

Maddie smiled. "Okay, sorry for waking you."

"No, you're not."

Maddie sat looking at her phone after ending the call. A sense of calm satisfaction washed over her. Never one to gamble on anything she felt that finally, she had found something, someone, worth taking a risk on.

∞ ∞ ∞

"Okay, so you take them three times a day after food and no alcohol," Maddie instructed as she guided her last patient of the morning out into the hall of the clinic. She sighed as she watched her leave. In spite of her initial reservations, Maddie was enjoying the role of a family doctor. Although she missed the hustle and bustle of the ER, she loved building a relationship with the people she treated. She turned to head back to her office when she spotted Alex leaving one of the examination rooms with one hand plunged into the pocket of her jacket.

Alex softly closed the door behind her and stepped into the hall. Her head shot up in surprise as Maddie said her name.

"Alex, are you okay? Is Jessica okay?" she asked quickly, gently taking her by the arm and guiding her into the office and closing the door behind them. "Has something happened?" Her eyes were wide with concern as she scanned Alex's face trying to decipher her reasons for being in the clinic.

Alex gave her a small smile. "I'm fine I just needed to see Mack."

Maddie frowned in concern. "Are you sick?"

"No, no. I..." She squeezed her eyes tight and gave an embarrassed sigh pulling her hand from her pocket.

"What?" Maddie gasped looking at the support that encased Alex's wrist. "What have you done?"

Alex furrowed her brow. "It's what we did that's the problem."

Gently cradling Alex's wrist, Maddie inspected the brace. "We?"

"I have tendonitis."

Maddie's eyes widened in response, and she pulled her lips into her mouth to quell the laughter that was starting to bubble up.

"Go on yuck it up," Alex groaned. "I blame you entirely, well sort of." she smiled. "I haven't had it for years, but it would appear that last night flared it up."

Maddie pulled her close. "I'm sorry. Are you free tonight? There's something I need to talk to you about."

Alex rested her chin on Maddie's shoulder. "I should be. I'll have Jessica though."

"That's okay. We can behave, especially since it looks like you're out of commission anyway," Maddie chuckled.

"There are other things I can do to you that don't require my hand," Alex whispered into Maddie's ear, smiling as her words received a shiver in response. "I'll see you tonight." She grinned, pulling away and walking back towards the door.

Maddie shook herself out of the reverie that Alex's whisper had placed her in. "I'll see you tonight." She smiled as Alex left before sitting back down behind her desk and pulling open her drawer. As she looked down at the contents, she gave a small laugh at the orange tippy cup still there from her first day in the clinic. She hooked her finger through one of the handles and brought it out, placing it on the desk in front of her. Tracing her fingers around the lid, she snorted softly as she remembered her reaction when Lou had presented it to her. She clenched her jaw and reached into the pocket of her white coat and pulled out her returned car keys. Leaning her elbows on the desk, she slipped her finger through the metal hoop and held them up to inspect them. A knock on the door roused her from her thoughts.

"You okay for your next patient?" Mack asked, poking her head around the door.

"Absolutely," Maddie replied pulling herself up and placing the cup and her keys into the desk drawer before closing it. "Tell them to come in."

∞ ∞ ∞

"Hey, Daddy Cool." Alex smiled as she straightened up and pushed her half-finished crossword to the side. "How was the first night at home with Ben?"

Peter smiled broadly. "Well, I've just dropped Ruth and 'Nighthawk' off at the clinic for a check-up, and I'm here for a bucket of coffee. Does that tell you how things went?"

Alex noticed the dark rings already around her friend's eyes. "Well, you're in the right place for a pick-me-up." She turned and started to pour a large cup of coffee.

Pulling the crossword puzzle around to face him, Peter started to check idly through clues that Alex had yet to solve. "Lou not in today?" he asked.

"Day off," Alex answered over her shoulder.

"So you're coming tonight?" he said, reaching for a pen to add a word to the puzzle.

Alex placed the coffee down in front of him. "Hey," she said, plucking the pen from Peter's fingers. "Tonight?" She lifted the puzzle and put it out of the mechanic's reach.

"Ben's sign ceremony." Peter frowned. "It's tonight in the bar, didn't Sully tell you?"

Clearing her throat, Alex shook her head. "Haven't seen Matt today, he dropped Jessica off at school this morning." She started to move cakes around on the display in the hope that looking busy would stop Peter from asking why there was a change to their usual schedule.

Peter took a long gulp of his coffee ignoring the heat of the liquid. "I thought that you usually had breakfast together on a Tuesday?"

"Not this morning," Alex said brightly. "About tonight. I have plans and Jessica."

Letting out a low growl of a yawn, Peter stretched up. "He's your godson, you can't skip it and bring Jessica, it's not like she's never sat in the bar before!" He drained his coffee with a satisfied lip smack. "I'm sure the good doctor won't mind sharing you with your friends for a bit," he added with a grin.

Alex felt her face flush. "Okay, we'll be there."

The bell above the door rang as Teddy opened it and Jessica burst in running to Peter for a twirl.

"Hey, big girl, you going to come see Ben tonight?" he asked spinning her around above his head.

Jessica gave a quick look over towards her mom who nodded. "Can I hold him?" she asked.

"If you're careful." Peter smiled planting a kiss on her cheek before lowering her to the ground.

"Hey, Daddy Cool," Teddy said, hugging Peter.

Pulling away, he pointed to Teddy and Alex. "You two need to stop hanging out." With that, he gave them a wave over his shoulder as he left the coffee shop to head towards the clinic.

Teddy gave Alex a quizzical look. "Why have we to stop hanging out?"

"We're speaking alike now." Alex laughed. "Kinda scary." She scooped her daughter into a hug. "How was school?" she asked, receiving a shrug in reply. Alex rolled her eyes. "There's a cookie in the kitchen for you and some milk." She swatted Jessica on the behind as she sprinted off towards the kitchen. "Be careful," she shouted after her. "How was school today?" she asked Teddy. "Did you behave?"

Teddy snatched a cookie from the plate on the display and shrugged. "It was school," she replied through a mouthful of cookie, catching falling crumbs with her fingertips. She looked up when she heard a soft snort coming from her friend. "Soooo you look..." Teddy rocked her head back and forward as she tried to place the look on Alex's face. Her eyes widened in recognition. "You got laid," she whispered. "I've seen that look...not for a while." She frowned. "But I have seen it."

Alex looked around the coffee shop glad that the afternoon rush had ended leaving the only other occupant sitting in the corner. "Shhhhh, seriously, Teddy!"

"But that's..." Teddy's smile fell from her face. "Wait." She started to count on her fingers, her head bobbing back and forth as she did. "It's brilliant!" she exclaimed finally satisfied that her Math added up.

"Okay, what was that?" Alex asked, pointing towards Teddy's hands. "Should I worry that you're in charge of my child's education and still use your fingers to count?"

Teddy scowled. "I was just trying to work out the days...and I win!" she said clapping her hands.

"Win what?" Alex asked, wiping the crumbs left by Teddy from the counter.

"The bet with Ruth. I said it would only take a week, she said two. I win since it was day seven when the doc and you finally got all Sapphic...wait, it did happen before midnight right? 'cause otherwise, I lose," Teddy asked, her face scrunching in concern.

Alex listened with her mouth hanging open. "Okay firstly." She held a finger up. "I can't believe you thought that I would have sex with someone I only knew for a week. You bet on me being easy!" She narrowed her eyes and glowered at Teddy. "And secondly, I'm not giving you any details about when, or where, or how."

Taking another cookie from the plate, Teddy sniffed haughtily as Alex stuck her head into the kitchen to check on Jessica. "Nineteen ninety-six, Spring break. You knew that girl less than four hours, and you slept with her!" she muttered.

Alex's head snapped back into the coffee shop, and she bore down on Teddy. "Nineteen ninety-four, you and Matt Sullivan on Peter's mother's lawn," she countered, pointing a finger at Teddy as she continued. "Just 'cause you did it then don't mean that you would..." She paused. "Wait, actually, Matt probably would." She grinned, swiping the cookie from Teddy's hand. "No pay, no eat."

Teddy grumbled pulling money from her pocket and slapping it on the counter before looking dolefully at Alex, who relented, and returned the cookie.

"I'm happy for you." Teddy smiled taking the cookie.

"I'm happy for me too." Alex beamed in response, her dimples crinkling her cheeks.

"I like the cut of her rug." Teddy mused. "Wait, is the saying cut of her jib?" She wrinkled her forehead in concentration. "'cause cut of her rug sounds wrong...and kinda dirty."

Alex rolled her eyes. "For the love of all things godly, stop with the cutting of the rug." She held up her hands hoping to stop Teddy from rambling further.

"What did you do to your wrist?" Teddy asked noticing the brace on Alex's wrist for the first time. "Actually second thought, sometimes there should be secrets in this town. Don't tell me." She shook her head and nibbled on her cookie.

∞ ∞ ∞

"So how did the first night at home go?" Maddie asked, handing Ben back to Ruth and jotting down his weight into his records.

"Looong, noisy, and tiring." Ruth smiled.

Maddie let out a small laugh. "I believe the response to that would be 'welcome to parenthood.' It's going to be like that for some time." They both looked up at the knock at the door and Peter's head appearing. "Ahh come in proud, Daddy." Maddie waved him in. "You look suitably exhausted."

"I have just downed a coffee like it was a tequila shot, I'm good for another twenty minutes," Peter replied, taking his son from his wife.

Maddie closed the file on the desk and rested her head in her hands taking a moment to observe the family sitting opposite her. Both parents were looking in awe at the tiny life they had created. She hoped that one day she would have that. She shook herself as her mind created an image of Alex looking at her, sitting with a baby in her arms. Resuming professional mode, she stood up.

"Keep an eye on his feeding. It's good he's latching on, just make sure that he's getting enough milk." She walked towards the door as Ruth and Peter stood up.

"You'll come to his sign ceremony tonight?" Ruth asked.

"Well, I..." Maddie hesitated. She didn't want to bail on Alex. She had to speak to her sooner rather than later about her plans.

"It's okay. I've spoken to Alex already. We'll see you both there at six, it won't be a late one." Peter smiled, catching his wife's surprised look when he mentioned Alex. "We'll be ready for bed at seven," he added looking down at his son. "Won't we?" he said in a baby voice, nuzzling against the side of his son's face.

Ruth narrowed her eyes and regarded the slightly embarrassed looking doctor. "So." She smiled. "We'll see you and Alex at six."

Maddie nodded, still surprised at Peter's words. "See you then." She smiled, closing the door behind them.

She was sitting completing her filing when Mack came into the office. "It would appear that the years of studying to be a nurse have been wasted on some of the inhabitants of this town, who appear to believe I'm your PA!" She held out a 'Post-it' under Maddie's nose.

Pulling her head back so she could focus on the writing on the yellow square, Maddie couldn't help but smile at the message, 'Have to go to the bar for Ben tonight, we'll pick you up. See you at yours at five thirty - Alex and Jessica'. She took the note from Mack. "I'm sure that Alex didn't mean anything by asking you to pass me this, she thinks a lot of you."

Mack raised an eyebrow. "I know that!" she snorted. "Her skinny blonde ass would have failed Biology in high school if it wasn't for me and our tutor sessions." She gave Maddie a smile and headed out backward from the office. "Haven't seen her tendonitis play up all of a sudden like that before." She chuckled as she closed the door.

Maddie palmed her hand against her forehead. "Jesus, this town!" she groaned.

Chapter Nine

At precisely five thirty there was a small knock at Maddie's door. She opened it and expected to see Alex looking back at her. Instead, she was looking down the empty path towards the gate.

"Hey, Maddie-Lyn," Jessica's voice rang out. Maddie looked down to where the small child was standing looking up at her with her mother's smile wide on her face.

"Hey, Jessica, where's your mom?" Maddie asked looking out.

"I'm here." Alex's voice sounded as she came into view around the side of the house. "I told you to wait," she scolded Jessica.

"I wanted to show Maddie-Lyn my dress." Jessica frowned at her mom.

Maddie bit her bottom lip at the adorableness of both mother and child. "It's a lovely dress, Jessica," Maddie said, pulling the door closed behind her and locking it. As she tossed the keys into her purse, the gleam of her car keys caught her eye. She silently cursed them for haunting her every move that day. She pushed her purse onto her shoulder as Jessica reached up and gripped her hand, before putting her other hand in her mother's.

"Do you like my mama?" Jessica asked innocently as they walked into town.

"*Jessica*!" Alex gasped. "Madeleine, I'm sorry...she—"

Maddie cut her off with a wave of her hand. "It's okay." She looked down at the girl. "Yes, Jessica, I like your mommy." She looked back up at Alex, who gave a bashful smile.

"How much?" Jessica asked.

"Well?" Maddie said cautiously, unsure how much to give away at this stage, particularly since she was talking to Alex's daughter.

“’cause my mama likes you enough to change her outfit five times,” Jessica said, skipping in between the two adults.

Alex rolled her eyes and prayed for the ground to swallow her, or her daughter, whole. At this point, she didn’t care which it was and would take whichever would make the embarrassment that she could feel flooding her face stop.

“You are so grounded, as soon as being grounded has some meaning,” she muttered.

Trying not to laugh Maddie looked back down at Jessica. “Well, in that case, I must like your mommy a lot ’cause I changed *six* times.” She leaned down and whispered in Jessica’s ear. “How do I look?”

Jessica gave her a quick look up and down. “You look like a vision,” she said, pleased with herself, then frowning slightly at the surprised response she got from the adults, immediately worrying that she’d said the wrong thing.

“Where’d you hear that, squirt?” Alex asked, changing the hand that held Jessica’s and placing an arm around her daughter’s shoulders.

“Daddy,” Jessica answered. “He said it to Aunt Lou when she came around last night.”

Alex raised her eyebrows and smirked at Maddie. “Did he now? Well, you’re right, Madeleine does look like a vision.” She gave Maddie a subtle wink.

They walked the rest of the way with Jessica rattling off what she’d done at school that day to Maddie. Alex listened intently as Maddie effortlessly chatted with Jessica about her day and elicited more information in the ten-minute walk than Alex had managed in the previous three months.

Reaching the bar, she held the door open as her daughter sped off to greet her father.

“She likes you,” she said quietly to Maddie, as she passed through the open door.

“I like her too.” Maddie smiled, squeezing Alex’s hand delicately as she passed by.

The bar was busy. It seemed to Maddie that the entire town had turned out for the ritual performed for all newborn Grace Falls inhabitants. Peter and Ruth were on the small stage with Ben. They smiled proudly as Sully presented them with a town sign; with the population number crossed out and increased by one. The room burst into applause as Peter accepted the sign then announced that drinks were on him. The announcement apparently took Ruth by surprise. She quickly scanned the packed bar in concern; calculating firstly how much Peter's generosity was going to cost them and then how she could get away with murdering him.

"Oh he's so going to pay for that later," Lou snorted, as she caught her sister's look.

"Yep," Teddy agreed. "Scotty, I'll have a double." She waved the glass towards Sully's bartender. "Might as well before she kills him," she reasoned, as Lou looked at her shocked.

"Me too Scotty," Lou said, holding her glass up.

Maddie was standing with Alex when she felt a buzzing in her purse. Frowning, she fumbled her hand through the contents until she located her cell. "Ah, I have to go take this," she said looking at Zoe's photo on caller ID. She pushed her purse back on her shoulder and made her way out of the main bar and into the small entranceway where the restrooms were located.

Alex spotted Lou standing at the bar with Teddy and made a beeline for her. "Hey, you. How's things?" she asked brightly.

"Good," Lou said, sipping her drink. "You?"

"Really good." Alex nodded, looking around her. "Enjoy your day off?"

Lou started to get slightly nervous at the tone of Alex's questioning. "Yep, was good," she answered carefully taking a drink.

"Excellent, I'm pleased. So I just wondered, were you doing the walk of shame from Matt's this morning when you saw Sam and sent him to Maddie's with a message for me?"

Lou spluttered her drink. "Hmm, sorry I...no idea what...excuse me." She put her glass on the bar and sped off towards the ladies' room.

Teddy grinned against the rim of her glass. "Well, that was just plain mean," she said, "and now you've done the bad cop, I'm off to be good cop and get the low down." She took a swig, put her glass down and headed off in hot pursuit of Lou.

Alex laughed as she watched her go. "Hey, Sam." She smiled and took a long suck at the straw in her drink as the mechanic approached the bar.

"Hey." He nodded. "The doc must be happy now her car's fixed," he said, waving trying to get the bartender's attention.

"Sorry?" Alex frowned, releasing the straw from her lips.

"Her car," Sam said, giving her a look as if she were dumb. "I dropped the keys off to her this morning. It's all fixed. Didn't she say?" He shrugged. "Did she tell you about the Sweet'N Low?" he whined, worrying that Alex didn't get the message from Lou.

"Yeah, I got the message," Alex said absently, looking towards the exit to where Maddie had disappeared on her phone call. A sinking feeling settled in her stomach as she realized now what Maddie wanted to talk to her about.

She was leaving.

Maddie sat in the toilet cubicle replaying the short conversation that she had just had with Zoe over in her mind. Her friend had called to check whether she had changed her mind and reverted to her original plan. She understood Zoe's concerns. She had never before done anything impulsively, even shopping for a new kitchen appliance required research, consumer reviews and various visits to shops, before she would make a purchase. Her lack of spontaneity had often been a source of argument in her relationship with Joanna. However, this time...this time, she was being spontaneous. She was going with her gut, and it honestly didn't feel like she was being rash. The notion that had started to take hold and grow made her feel a warmth inside.

She felt at home.

She felt almost giddy at the thought. Until she had spoken to Zoe that morning, it had been just that, a thought. Now that thought was slowly being put into action. She would call the chief at the hospital tomorrow and withdraw from the position. When she had left the clinic that night, she told Mack that she needed to speak to Timothy. She wanted to talk to him about becoming the full-time doctor in Grace Falls. She had to bite her lips to stop herself from laughing aloud.

She heard the bathroom door open, and someone enter and let out a loud exhale of breath. The door opened again.

"So you and Sully?"

Maddie's eyes narrowed as she recognized Teddy's voice.

"Yes...me and Sully," Lou responded. "God, can you keep nothing quiet in this town?"

"You were the one that told Sam to give Maddie a message for Alex. How'd you know that she was there anyway? I only found out that they did the deed this afternoon."

Lou checked her eye makeup in the mirror of the restroom. "Jessica said that Alex was taking dinner over to the doc. Plus there was no-one at Alex's when I called around this morning, which is when I saw Sam. Do you know he was fixing that car through the night?"

Teddy leaned against the sink. "Serves him right, with his idiot idea. Does that mean the car is fixed now?" she asked, thinking about how upset Alex was going to be once Maddie left. Her heart ached for her friend; it had been so long since she had seen her this happy.

"Hey, that idiot idea made sure we had a doctor in town while my sister gave birth to my nephew. So I, for one, am glad that Sam lied about them having the parts, and don't forget all the other people she saw and helped this week." Lou's head twitched as she said the word week. "Hey, she's been here a week. Does that mean you won?"

Teddy beamed. "It does, I should go get my winnings from your sister."

Lou laughed. She had seen Maddie gently probe for information on Alex and the glances that had been exchanged during Sunday dinner at Ruth's. She smiled as she thought about the atmosphere that surrounded the two women when they were together. The attraction that coursed between the two was almost palpable. "I thought it might have taken a little longer."

Pulling open the door, Teddy waved her hand for Lou to go first. "Yeah well, I know the Milne charm first hand, even though Alex complained earlier for saying she was easy." Lou walked out of the bathroom followed by Teddy.

Maddie could hear Teddy's voice ask another question about Sully before the door swished shut and silenced it.

Hot angry tears poured down her face. She felt used and humiliated. The warmth and generosity of the town had been built on a lie, all because they wanted a doctor. They had lied about her car, keeping her a relative hostage in the town, playing with her. But worse than that, worse than anything she'd ever experienced was hearing that she had been part of the town's entertainment, that her time with Alex was part of some elaborate bet, and Alex, a loud sob escaped as she crumpled against the wall of the cubicle, Alex regarded her as easy. Hearing that word applied to her, regardless of context, took her back twelve months to the restaurant and Joanna ending their relationship because it seemed like Maddie just wanted an easy life. She wiped angrily at the tears, took a deep breath, and stood up. This is where impulsiveness got her, this is where spontaneity got her. She'd wound up being toyed with and slapped soundly in the face by it.

Timothy McNeil was running late. He was sure that he would have missed the sign being handed over but wanted to go and wish the young family well. He pulled open the door to the bar and was practically bundled over by Maddie as she barged out of ladies' room and out of the building. "Doctor Marinelli, I was hoping you would be here. Mack mentioned that you wanted to speak to me?" His smile faded as he spotted the tears streaming from Maddie's eyes. "You okay?" he asked, full of concern.

"I'm fine," Maddie replied monotone. "I wanted to let you know that my car is fixed and I'm leaving immediately. Could you thank Mack for me, she's been wonderful." She put her hand to her mouth to smother the sob that was bubbling in her throat and turned to run towards Peter's Auto Shop.

Timothy watched her leave then, pursing his lips, he entered the bar. He greeted familiar faces and exchanged pleasantries as he made his way to the bar. "Ladies." He greeted Lou, Teddy, and Alex. "Can I buy you a drink?"

They gave him their order, and he signaled the bartender across to pass it on. "So," he said, turning his attention back to the three women. "Such a shame our doc is leaving us."

Teddy immediately looked at Alex, concerned at her reaction.

"You never know, maybe she's found something worth staying for," Lou said, looking over at Alex, who was studying her feet.

"I wish that were true, but she seemed pretty determined when she left here a moment ago." Timothy shrugged, handing money over to Scotty in exchange for their drinks.

"What?" Alex's head shot up. "What do you mean?"

"I just saw her, damn near knocked me on my ass she came out the restroom so fast," he replied, taking a sip of his soda.

Teddy and Lou flashed each other a horrified look.

"Oh my God." Teddy gasped. "Alex, we're sorry, she must have heard us."

"Heard you?" Alex narrowed her eyes. "Heard you say what exactly?"

Lou started to flap her hands nervously. "We were talking about me and Sully. So not important at this moment," she added, seeing Alex's temper flash in her eyes. "And how Sam and Peter lied about having her car parts so there would be a doctor here for Ruth."

Alex's eyes widened as she heard this for the first time. "What?"

Teddy placed a hand on Alex's arm. "She also would have heard us talk about the bet I made with Ruth. I'm sorry," she apologized. Her eyes were full of remorse as she saw her friend visibly shrink with this piece of information.

"I've got to go speak to her." Alex pushed past them. "Look after Jessica," she called, as she weaved her way through the bar-goers towards the door.

∞ ∞ ∞

Maddie zipped up her hold-all. She had rushed around the house, opening drawers and lifting their contents wholesale into the bag. Clothes had been ripped from hangers, rolled up into a ball, and thrust into the bag. She had swept her toiletries with one hand off the shelf and into the waiting wash-bag. She swung the hold-all over her shoulder and picked up the last of her boxes that had been sitting in the hallway for the past week, and headed down towards her car. She slammed the trunk closed and made her way towards the driver's door. She had just opened it as she heard her name being called from behind her.

"Madeleine, wait."

She turned as Alex ran towards her.

"Please wait, don't go...not like this."

Shaking her head, Maddie slammed the door closed. "Really, how would you like me to go. Is there some bet on about when I'll leave? Or is there something else that I'm needed for in this town that you've been sent to lure me back for?" she spat.

"I didn't know," Alex pleaded, tears starting to well in her eyes. "I didn't know about the car, honestly."

"In the town with no secrets, you expect me to believe that you didn't know that!" Maddie said sarcastically, shaking her head angrily. "Credit me with some intelligence, Alex."

Alex grabbed her wrist. "I didn't, I promise."

"What about the bet between Teddy and Ruth?" Maddie asked, hesitating, wanting to believe Alex with every ounce of her being. She saw shame flash across Alex's face as she lowered her eyes. "Thought so." Maddie shook her head and shrugged off Alex's hand.

"It wasn't the way you think," Alex cried.

Maddie yanked the car door open and tossed the keys to the Anderson house onto the sidewalk at Alex's feet. She flung herself in and roared the car into life as she gunned the engine and drove off. She looked in her rearview mirror at the figure of Alex standing outside the gate of the Anderson house. Her arms were wound tightly around herself.

Squeezing her eyes closed to rid herself of the sight, Maddie sped out of Grace Falls.

∞ ∞ ∞

"We didn't say anything to Alex 'cause she would have told her!" Sam argued, several pairs of eyes swung around towards him. "You know she would have." He shrugged.

Teddy sighed. "It doesn't matter now, you both need to apologize to the doc," she instructed, pointing at Sam and Peter. Then, looking towards Ruth, she sighed. "And we need to as well." The shame she felt coated her tone.

Ruth exhaled slowly. "Yeah, we do," she replied sadly.

Their discussion was halted at the sound of an engine roaring through the town. They all looked up out of the window of the bar waiting for whatever was making the noise to pass. The sight of a blue T-Bird whirring past was greeted with a collective groan.

"Well that's not good," Teddy mused, as they exchanged worried glances. Then with a quirk of her eyebrow, Teddy straightened herself up. "Jessica!" she yelled looking around for the young girl. "C'mon, squirt. I'm taking you home."

Alex watched, frozen to the spot, as Maddie's car disappeared into the distance. She stood long after the car had left the town's boundaries and was heading northwards towards the interstate. Eventually, she let her head drop and closed her eyes as tears fell from them landing softly on the sidewalk. Heaving in a deep breath, she swallowed the lump in her throat and bent down to pick up the keys nestled between her feet. She inspected them in her open palm, before tightening her fist around them. Giving one last look towards the road, she turned and walked towards her home, her shoulders slumped, and head bowed.

Chapter Ten

The rooms in Alex's house were eerily silent as Teddy and Jessica entered.

"Where's my mama?" Jessica asked, looking up at her aunt.

"I'm not sure, why don't we go look for her. You look upstairs and while you're there get your PJs on. I'll look out this way." Teddy smiled ushering Jessica up the stairs.

Teddy had a fairly good idea where Alex would be but still gave the living room and den a cursory glance. "Marco," she yelled, smiling as she heard a weak 'Polo' shouted in response. She opened the kitchen door and pushed open the fly screen. Her head flopped to the side, and she exhaled slowly at the sight of her friend huddled under a comforter on the swing seat.

"Hey," she said softly.

Alex looked up. Her blue eyes were rimmed with red. "She's gone," she said simply, her bottom lip quivering.

"I guessed." Teddy sat down beside her. "I'm so sorry." She placed a comforting hand on her friend's knee.

Alex shook her head. "What were they thinking?"

"That Ruth was about to give birth and that it would be better to have a doctor in town when that happened. We all know how important that was when Jessica was born." She pulled her friend into a hug. "I can tell you what wasn't going through their minds. Nor for one minute would they have thought that you would end up getting hurt." She kissed Alex's head. "They couldn't legislate for the fact that you Milne kids' crap charisma and that you and she would, *you know*, or that you'd let yourself fall for someone after all this time."

The fingers on Alex's one free hand plucked aimlessly at the comforter. "I know." She sniffed. "You and Ruth didn't help," she said accusingly.

"No, we didn't," Teddy replied honestly. "And I'm sorry for that, but you know that we didn't mean anything, *anything,* by it. We bet on everything. There's a sweepstake about when they think I'll have sex next on the go that I'm not meant to know about."

Alex gave a small snort, then sighed. "She looked at me like she didn't know me." Her words came out cracked with a soft sob.

Teddy pushed her friend's chin up so she could look in her eyes. "And if she thought you were complicit in any of this, then she doesn't know you, sweetie."

"You found her!" Jessica yelled, running towards her mother.

Alex forced a smile. "Hey, squirt, you're all ready for bed."

Jessica pulled herself onto her mother's lap. "Yup, can I have a story?"

Teddy caught Alex's eye as she snuggled her face into her daughter's hair.

"How about I get story duty tonight. Your mama hogs you too much." Teddy smiled, standing up and slipping her hands around Jessica's sides to gently lift her. Jessica flung her arms around her aunt's neck and nestled her head under Teddy's chin. "You're getting way too big for this, squirt." Teddy groaned tightening her hold on the child. "And while we're going upstairs you can tell me about how much time your Aunt Lou is spending at your daddy's," she said, waggling her eyebrows towards Alex over Jessica's shoulder.

Alex let out a half laugh as she watched her friend and daughter disappear into the house. She then let out a sad sigh as she turned back and looked towards the empty Anderson house. She shuffled her shoulders slightly and jerked the hand that was tucked under the comforter until she freed it from its confines. She looked down at her open fist. Deep red marks scored her palm from the tight grip she'd maintained on the keys that still sat in her hand.

"Madeleine," she whispered sadly.

∞ ∞ ∞

"Maddie-Lyn says she's going to draw a skeleton with me and name all of the bones," Jessica enthused after Teddy had read the obligatory story.

Teddy's hand paused as she slipped the book back onto the bookshelf. She pushed it back in place then turned to face Jessica, who was now lying down under her duvet. "Sweetie, I'm really sorry, but Maddie has had to go," she said, sitting down on the edge of Jessica's bed.

"Where? Why?" The young girl's face crunched up in confusion. "She promised!"

"I know, and I'm sure that she had every intention on keeping that promise." Teddy smiled, brushing Jessica's hair from her face. "But she was only ever here because she was on her way to San Francisco to work when her car broke down and now Sam and your Uncle Peter have fixed it she's had to go."

Jessica's blue eyes looked up at her aunt. "But she liked Mama. She said so." Jessica's hand reached out and dragged a teddy under the duvet. "Enough to change *six* times."

Teddy cupped Jessica's cheek. "And I'm sure she still likes your mama, but she wasn't ever going to stay."

"I wanted her to. Mama laughed a lot around her and flicked her hair."

Reaching down to place a kiss on Jessica's forehead, Teddy sighed. "We all wanted her to stay, squirt, but sometimes people have to go."

"Like Uncle Bear?" Jessica asked, referring to her uncle that she only knew from photographs and from stories her mom told her.

Teddy's breath caught in her throat. "Yeah, just like Uncle Bear. You get some sleep, and I'll help you with your skeleton. I know the names of at least four bones since I've broken them."

Jessica gave her a skeptical look. "Okay, but you can't make stuff up if you don't know. I'm not a baby anymore."

Switching the light off, Teddy laughed. "I know that. squirt and I promise I won't make stuff up." She closed the door and rested her back against it.

She hadn't expected Jessica to bring up Bear in the conversation. Most folks avoided speaking about him, particularly to her, as it dredged up too much emotion. When, after they graduated high school, Alan Milne had ended their relationship and announced that he had enlisted in the Marines, Teddy had been distraught. Her dreams of settling down with him after college in Grace Falls had disappeared with that one conversation.

She, like Alex, left the town for college, returning only during holidays. She dated other boys while away and had that now infamous tryst with Sully on Peter's mom's lawn while drunk. But through it all, she was in love with Bear. When she realized this, she'd taken a bus and stood outside his base to tell him. From that moment on their relationship rekindled. She had finished her education and became a supply teacher so she could have the freedom to move to wherever he was based and, for five years, their relationship continued. Throughout that time, she waited on him asking her to marry him. It was a question that she would never hear from his lips. She'd been there to wave him off when he left for Afghanistan and only two months later was standing next to Alex in a hanger as his body was lifted off of a plane.

When Alex called her to tell her the news of his death, she was devastated. A devastation that only deepened when she read the letter that Bear had left for her should he be killed. In it he told her that he wanted to marry her and have children with her, but not while he was in the Marines. He'd seen the impact of being a Marine's wife first-hand; his father's absence effectively leaving his mother to raise their children single-handedly. He had been saving money and wanted to return to Grace Falls with her and open a coffee shop. He had wanted something easy where he could forget that he'd been in the military and it was to be called Ruby's after his grandma. However, the September events in New York meant that he had to delay that plan in order to perform his duty. He apologized in his letter that he would never get the chance to dance at their wedding or kiss their children goodnight.

After losing Bear, she'd returned to Grace Falls, taken a job in the local school and given Alan's money to Alex with instructions to open a coffee shop.

Teddy bit at her bottom lip, tamping down the familiar grief that made her chest ache, and headed downstairs to Alex. Her wounds were old, and it would serve no purpose to pick at the scars. Tonight was about fresh wounds, and there was no doubt in Teddy's mind that Alex was hurting. Despite the brevity of her time with Maddie, the spark that had been missing in Alex for a long time had returned. Teddy had felt a warmth in her own chest at the thought that perhaps there could be a time of happiness ahead for her. She picked up a bottle of Jim Beam as she walked through the house back towards the porch swing seat where she and her best friend had spent many an hour setting the world to rights.

"Thought I'd bring the only man in your life out." Teddy smiled, holding up the bottle and two glasses.

Alex wiped the tears from her face and looked up managing a weak smile. "What do you call Matt?"

"He doesn't count. He's not a man. He's still a kidult," Teddy replied, sitting down on the swing and handing Alex a glass. She poured them both hearty measures, then put the bottle on the wooden porch and held up her glass. As Alex clinked hers against it, Teddy grinned. "'tis better to have loved and lost, than never to have loved at all."

Alex growled. "Tennyson was talking out of his ass when he wrote that, and you need to stop quoting him at me."

"Yup." Teddy smiled against the rim of her glass. "He definitely was."

∞ ∞ ∞

Maddie pulled into the parking lot of a twenty-four-hour motel. Her eyes were sore and grainy from crying, and her body ached from the five hours of continual driving since she had left Grace Falls. She checked in and wearily climbed the stairs to her allocated room with her hold-all and doctor's bag in her hand. She stumbled into the room and flipped the light switch on. Tired eyes examined the anonymous room where she would spend the night. She gave a sigh and kicked the door closed behind her, dumping her bags onto the floor.

Walking past the mirror she avoided her reflection, knowing that if the guy's reaction behind the desk at the motel was anything to go by, then the hours of sobbing as she'd driven had more than taken their toll. She switched the shower on and slowly peeled her clothes off until she stood naked. Numbly she climbed into the shower and let the hot water wash away the traces of the day. A fresh wave of tears started as her mind thought back to the shower that she'd started the day with.

She dried herself on autopilot then wrapped the towel around her while she sourced something to sleep in from her bag. Dressed in her pajamas she listlessly switched on the TV, flipping through the channels willing something to appear that would stop her brain from thinking. Unable to focus, she switched off the TV and lay in the dark. Suddenly she became aware that the incessant beeping that she could hear coming from her doctor's bag.

The beeping became louder as she popped the latches and opened her bag. She rolled her eyes and sighed audibly as she located the source of the noise. The brick of a cell phone that Mack had given her was still in her bag and beeping to tell her that there was a message. She dialed the number of the answering service and put the phone to her ear. Her heart rate increased as she waited to hear whose voice had left her a message.

"You've stolen the damn bat phone," Mack's voice yelled. "I heard you've gone"—her voice softened—"and I wanted to say that I'm sorry, that you've gone 'cause I've enjoyed working with you."

Maddie sniffed and chewed on her lips.

"And, that you're a fool if the rumors are right and you think that Alex had anything to do with those idiot ideas. I've known her since she and that devil of a brother of hers moved here when they were ten, and she doesn't have a malicious bone in her body, and for that matter, I've known Peter Campbell since he was a hundred and ten pounds and had a white boy afro. We played in band together, and he's not the kind of man to like lying to you. Sam, on the other hand, was an All-State wrestler, and he took a lot of blows to the head. What I'm trying to say is...if you're goin' 'cause you're all up about being a doctor in a big city hospital then okay. But if you're running 'cause you think people here don't care 'bout you, then you're dumber than you look. Post my damn phone back," she finished.

Maddie sat listening to the static on the line as the message clicked off. She sat for several minutes before dropping the phone into her bag and pulling out her own cell and typing the message '*Back to plan A, will be with you tomorrow night.*' She pressed send then flopped back on the bed.

∞ ∞ ∞

Alex lay awake staring at the ceiling above her bed. Her fingers, clasped against her chest, were tapping furiously against the back of each hand. She was done being upset about what happened, now she was working herself up into a tizzy. Her jaw worked as she ground her teeth thinking about how annoyed she was with Maddie and the situation and what she wanted to tell the doctor about her reaction to it.

"I can actually hear you think!" Teddy grumbled, twisting until she lay on her stomach. She propped herself on her elbows and rubbed her grainy eyes until she could focus on her best friend. "I stayed so I could get some sleep and now what with the tapping and the grinding that you're doing, and that's just the noise from your brain, I can't sleep!"

"You stayed 'cause we drank the best part of that bottle, and you couldn't see your finger in front of your nose," Alex countered, "and you could have stayed in the spare room. You were the one that insisted on sleeping in here."

Teddy rolled her eyes. "I don't like sleeping in Bear's room," she mumbled, positioning her arms under her pillow and flopping down. She kept her face turned towards Alex. "So what's going on?"

"I'm mad," Alex growled, turning to face Teddy and resting her head on her hand. "She didn't even give me a chance to defend myself. She just took off. I mean who does that?"

Lifting her chin, Teddy looked into Alex's eyes. "You know when Bear first enlisted, he said all the teenagers were excited, everything was new and different. It was an adventure."

Alex frowned wondering what her friend was trying to say.

"Then when he got older, he said you could spot the guys that had seen conflict. You could see it in their eyes. The sheen was gone; they had grown up. They carried scars."

"I don't—" Alex started, her mouth hanging open as Teddy shushed her.

"And then he said you could see the guys who were older and who had seen more. They were acutely aware of their own mortality and what they had to lose. For some, the slightest noise or movement would take them right back to relive their experiences."

Alex blinked. "Are you comparing what she did to PTSD?" she asked incredulously.

Teddy snuggled against her pillow. "None of us are getting any younger, Alex and we all carry around scars of previous relationships, maybe she has PRSD. Post Relationship Stress Disorder," she clarified when she saw Alex frown. She thought back to the previous evening when Jessica had mentioned Bear. "A look or a set of circumstances can scratch a scar, or sometimes blow a freaking big hole! What I'm saying is that maybe what she heard sparked something and that wasn't necessarily related to you."

"You think I shouldn't be angry?" Alex asked, laying her head down on her pillow and considering Teddy's words.

"I think that you"—Teddy pursed her lips thoughtfully—"I think that you shouldn't look back with regret. It happened, and you should take the positives from it. You allowed yourself to like someone and, yeah, you don't know what was going on in her head"—Teddy opened her mouth wide to stop Alex interrupting her—"An' she should have used her words rather than driving out of here like a bat out of hell, but what's done is done."

Alex rolled onto her back again and looked up at the ceiling. "So what're your triggers?" she asked quietly. "Your PRSD?"

Teddy snorted quietly. "Where do I begin?"

They lay quietly for a while. Teddy felt herself start to doze off again when Alex's voice broke the silence. "I don't think I have any," she said, turning her head to look at Teddy. "Triggers I mean. I've been laying here thinking, and I don't have any." She turned her head back again and closed her eyes, allowing her brain to finally close off.

Teddy opened one eye and started to sing quietly, "*Strumming my pain with his fingers. Singing my life with his words. Killing me softly with his song, killing me softly with his song, telling my whole life with his words. Killing me softly with his song.*" She bobbed her head to an imaginary beat as she impersonated the intro. "Beeeeong beeeong beeeong."

"Oh God." Alex groaned. "Okay, so the Fugees may be a trigger."

Smiling to herself Teddy closed her eye again. "One time," she murmured, earning a slap from Alex.

∞ ∞ ∞

Maddie pulled the handle of her bag further onto her shoulder and raised her fist to rap on the door. She examined the hallway as she waited on the white door being opened. She could hear footsteps against the hardwood floor on the other side of the door before it finally opened. She was greeted by her friend dressed in a long-sleeved grey T-shirt and baggy checked pajama bottoms.

"Hi," Maddie said timidly. "I'm sorry it took me longer than I thought."

Pushing the door open wider, Zoe moved out of the way to let Maddie enter. "It's okay, you're here now." She reached down and took the bags from Maddie's hands. "C'mon in. There's coffee brewing, or I have wine if you need something with a kick."

"Wine please," Maddie replied wearily.

She followed Zoe into the loft apartment that was to be her new home. Zoe dumped the bags on the sofa then called out from the kitchen, "Red or white?"

"White please," Maddie replied, flopping on the sofa.

"So?" Zoe returned with two glasses of wine. "What happened?" she asked, handing Maddie a glass.

Maddie opened her mouth to speak. However, words eluded her, and she shrugged as large teardrops fell from her eyes into her wine.

"Oh, sweetie," Zoe soothed, taking the glass from Maddie's hand and wrapping her arms around her friend. "You don't have to tell me tonight. You look whacked. Why don't I show you to your room?" Maddie nodded against her friend's shoulder and allowed Zoe to pull her from the sofa. "I haven't unpacked your boxes. I just sort of stacked them in the corner," Zoe said apologetically.

"Thank you," Maddie replied almost mechanically.

"I'll leave you to get some sleep," Zoe murmured as she pulled her friend into another tight hug. "I'm just down the hall if you need anything." She gave Maddie's shoulder a supportive rub then left her standing in her new room.

Maddie stood still, looking at the closed door that Zoe had just exited through. She sighed and gave her new bedroom a cursory once-over. Her space now consisted of a large dark wood bed, a tall chest of drawers and a wardrobe. She walked over to her boxes and moved them aside until she located the one that she wanted. Pulling at the brown tape sealing it closed, she opened the box, reached inside, and pulled out a thick blanket. She smiled as she felt its familiar touch under her fingers as she ran her palm over the different textures. From her teens wherever Maddie lived, her blanket went with her and made her feel as though she were home. She laid the blanket onto the duvet then sat down on the edge of the bed.

"Home sweet home," she murmured, pressing her lips together. She slowly flopped back onto the bed and breathed deeply closing her eyes tightly. "Home sweet home."

∞ ∞ ∞

The sound of activity in the main living area and the gentle waft of coffee woke her. Rubbing her eyes, she realized that she had fallen asleep still dressed in the clothes that she'd driven in and her shoes. She gave an exploratory sniff and decided that the shower would have to wait until she had inhaled some coffee and brought up the remainder of her belongings that she had left in the trunk of her car. She pulled open her bedroom door and walked hesitantly out into the apartment.

"Coffee?" Zoe asked as Maddie padded into the kitchen.

"Please," Maddie replied.

"You're looking much better this morning," Zoe remarked, handing over a mug of coffee and perching on one of the stools. "So what happened? I thought that you were going native?"

Maddie turned her attention from looking longingly towards the delicious smelling coffee. "Yeah...I"—she paused, thinking about her time in Grace Falls—"I guess that being impetuous doesn't suit me." She laughed bitterly. "God, Zoe, I honestly thought that I had found something." She shook her head to rid her mind of what she had hoped that she had found. Something that her previous relationship had promised but failed spectacularly to deliver. "But, really, I mean who in their right mind would throw away their specialty, that they've worked their ass off for, to switch to family medicine?"

"Well I did wonder," Zoe said cautiously, taking a sip of her coffee. "I mean you're such a city girl. What the hell could a hick town in the middle of nowhere offer you?" She waved her hand dismissively, trying to perk her friend up. "Apart from poison ivy and snake bites," she added.

Maddie gave a sad smile at Zoe's assessment. For a moment her defenses dropped, and she was in Ruby's Coffee Shop, surrounded by the smell of the coffee being brewed. She could see Alex standing behind the counter wiping her hands on a towel as she laughed at something being said. Her dimples would be creasing her cheeks, and her blonde hair would be tugged back into a messy ponytail with curls escaping around her face. She swallowed hard at the lump forming in her throat.

"Maddie?" Zoe said gently. "I asked you what you wanted for breakfast."

"God...sorry I was miles away." Maddie apologized. She brought her coffee to her lips for a careful sip.

Zoe held up her mug as if toasting Maddie. "Well, you're here now...Welcome to San Francisco."

Chapter Eleven

Two weeks later...

Alex took in a deep breath and rolled over. She opened one eye slightly towards the direction of the clock on the nightstand. Both eyes sprang open as she registered the time on the display.

"Crap!" she exclaimed, pushing the covers off her she leaped from the bed. "Jessica! Honey, get up! We're late."

She ran into her bathroom and stripped off her nightclothes. Grabbing her deodorant, she opted for the shower in a can approach to her ablutions. Running naked through her room to her closet, with her toothbrush in her mouth, she listened for movement in her daughter's room. Hearing nothing, she pulled her toothbrush out and yelled encouragement, "Jessica...Up...Now!"

Alex yanked on her underpants and shimmied into a pair of jeans, then raced around with the button and belt undone as she tried to locate her bra. She quickly put it on and grabbed a T-shirt. Pulling it over her head and getting it snagged with her toothbrush, she cursed softly as her head eventually popped through. She ran to the bathroom and spat out the toothpaste, throwing her toothbrush after it into the sink.

Storming down the hall, Alex pulled her hair into a ponytail as she wobbled her feet into her sneakers. "Jessica, you... oh." She looked surprised at the sight of her fully dressed daughter sitting on the floor drawing. "You're ready."

Jessica looked up and smiled.

"Well, come on. Let's get you to school or your Aunt Teddy will kill me."

"Miss Roosevelt," Jessica corrected. "She's Miss Roosevelt at school and Aunt Teddy at home."

Sighing, Alex rolled her eyes. "Well, Miss Roosevelt will kill me, so get a wriggle on." She ushered her daughter out of the door, frowning as she saw the pile of paper that she had been drawing on. Each page had drawings of skeletons or bones.

"Can I have breakfast?" Jessica asked as she shrugged her backpack on.

"You can have a banana, squirt, that's all we've time for." Alex tossed the fruit in Jessica's direction before hastily fastening the brown leather belt around her waist. She picked up the keys to the coffee shop and headed towards the front door. "Hup to it," she called over her shoulder as she went.

"Mama, can you sign my permission slip?" Jessica asked, waving a scrunched up piece of paper. "We're going to the Falls tomorrow."

Alex huffed out as she grabbed a pen from the small table beside the door. "Now you ask! You had all last night," she complained, scrawling her signature onto the folded paper. She thrust the paper back towards her daughter who tucked it into her pocket. "Now can we go?" she asked with her eyebrows raised, as she pointed through the open door. Jessica skipped past her mother, and Alex closed the door behind them.

Jessica turned as she entered the door to the school and waved to her mom, who was standing watching from the sidewalk. Teddy raised her eyebrows and pointed to her watch in mock anger. Alex held her hands out and raised her shoulders in apology before letting out a long breath and heading towards the coffee shop.

∞ ∞ ∞

"Are you even listening to me?" Lou waved a hand in front of Alex's face.

Shaking her head slightly Alex turned to focus on her assistant. "Huh? Sorry, what did you say?" She frowned, trying to recall if she had registered Lou's words.

"I said. We're running low on marshmallows, you need to add them to the supplier's list." Lou narrowed her eyes, "Were you thinking about her again?"

"What? No!" Alex shook her head indignantly. "At least not today, no." She gave a small smile. "No, I'm worried that Jessica is going through another death obsession."

Lou's top lip twitched. "Oh God please not again."

The last time Jessica had become interested in mortality it had unfortunately coincided with the death of Ruth and Lou's mother the previous year.

As both regarded it as a normal part of life, Alex and Sully had decided to let her attend the funeral due to her inquisitiveness around the subject. As parents, they both wanted to shield her from hurt, but they had agreed early on that they would be as honest with her as possible. However, no-one was prepared for her young voice to ring out during a quiet point in the burial, announcing that she 'Couldn't see anything and was Mrs. Anderson in the ground yet?' Fortunately, Ruth had a rather dark sense of humor and had seen the funny side. Lou on the other hand was more sensitive in nature and had taken Jessica's approach to death somewhat personally.

"She's been drawing skeletons for weeks and keeps asking about bones. She fell out with Teddy over the funny bone."

Lou snorted. "She's never forgiven Teddy for telling her that electricity came from a giant glow worm's ass."

Alex laughed. "Nope, she still brings that up on a regular basis."

The door opened, and the ringing of the bell above signaled a customer. Both women looked up in greeting.

"Afternoon."

"Afternoon, Mack," they called out simultaneously.

"Haven't seen you for a while," Alex remarked, pouring out Mack's usual drink.

The small nurse let out a long sigh and her lips twisted. "No doctor to replace Marinelli, so I'm commuting back to St Anton again. We're thinking of moving there. It don't matter none to Harvey since he works county-wide, but I can't do the commute with Lewis at school here, it's not fair on him."

Alex passed a mug of coffee and reached her hand out, placing it on top of Mack's. "I'm sorry."

"Not your fault the one doctor that people seemed to like took off," Mack replied, hoping that Alex believed that she wasn't responsible for Maddie's departure. The door opened again, and Jessica entered the coffee shop. Mack turned towards her with a wide smile on her face. "Well look at you. Have you grown?" she asked, pulling the girl into a hug.

"I'm almost the same height as you!" Jessica replied, wrapping her arms around Mack's waist as far as she could.

Mack snorted. "Well, that's not a whole lot to aspire to." She cupped Jessica's face, so they were looking into each other's eyes. "Do you know what these are?" she asked, holding her hands up.

Jessica grinned, knowing the response to the often-asked question. "The first hands to ever touch me."

Alex smiled softly to herself as she listened to the conversation. Inwardly, her mind recalled the times she'd heard her grandmother ask the same question to a number of Grace Falls residents.

"And?" Mack asked, her eyes wide and a smirk on her lips.

"The first ones to smack me if I get out of line," Jessica answered, bouncing on her tiptoes. "Mama," Jessica said, turning to look at her mother. "Daddy is outside waiting. He wants some Rocky Road."

Alex raised an eyebrow. "And he sent you in?" She looked out of the window to where Sully was hovering, he grinned goofily and waved through the window. "Tell him that sending you in doesn't get him extra," she told her daughter, her eyes narrowed in mock anger. She pulled out a bag and started to fill it with pieces of Rocky Road, putting in a couple of additional slabs. Twirling it around to seal it, she handed it across to her daughter and leaned over the counter for a kiss. "I'll see you tomorrow, squirt, behave at your Daddy's."

"I will," Jessica said, taking the bag.

"I'll pick you up from school tomorrow," Alex called after her departing daughter.

"It's okay." Jessica stopped and spun around. "Aunt Teddy will drop me off here, after our trip."

"Right. I forgot. Behave," she yelled as Jessica disappeared out the door.

"I can't believe how big she is now," Mack murmured, taking a sip of her coffee.

"Me neither." Alex smiled.

∞ ∞ ∞

The following afternoon Alex was in the kitchen when she heard the door to the coffee shop open, she heard Teddy's voice asking for a drink. Wiping her hands on a towel, she left what she was doing to go see her daughter. She was used to the co-parenting arrangement that she and Sully had developed over time. However, the nights when Jessica was with her dad always seemed to drag for Alex.

Teddy had a large bright smile on her face when she walked into the shop. "Hey, Alex." She smiled in greeting. "How's things?"

Alex gave her a confused look. "Good, where's Jessica?"

Teddy's quirked her eyebrows quizzically. "Did Sully not contact you? He sent me a text this morning to say she was sick and wouldn't be in school."

"No, he hasn't. That's a shame, she would have been disappointed to miss the trip," Alex replied, digging her phone out of her pocket to call Sully.

"What trip?" Teddy asked, her face scrunched in confusion.

Alex hesitated. About to hit Sully's contact details, her thumb paused in midair. "The trip that you were taking them on to the Falls today. I signed a permission slip," she said slowly. Her concern was starting to build.

Teddy shook her head slowly. "I wasn't taking the kids to the Falls today, or any other day."

"Shit," Alex gasped, her thumb punching down on Sully's contact details.

Teddy and Lou shared nervous looks as she paced back and forth waiting for him to answer. "Matt, is Jessica with you?" she asked quickly. Her face fell at his response. "Did you text Teddy this morning to say she was sick and staying off school?" Her hand gripped the counter for support. "Matt, you need to come to Ruby's now. She wasn't in school today. I think she's gone," Alex said, her voice hitching as she spoke. She hung the call up and placed her other hand on the counter, trying to steady her breathing. "He said that he left her at the corner before the school, she was walking in with Lucy."

Teddy pulled out her cell and selected a number. "Hi, Mary, it's Teddy. Hi, listen I need you to ask Lucy about Jessica; she was walking with her to school this morning, and Jessica never made it in." She nodded as she listened to Mary speak, her eyes never leaving Alex's, she covered the phone. "She's going to ask...Hi," she said, removing her hand. "She's sure?" Teddy's entire body slumped. "Okay, thanks." She hung up the phone. Her mouth opened as if she couldn't process the words that were about to come out. "Lucy said she saw her get into a black car."

A sob escaped Alex. She felt Lou's arms tighten around her and guide her towards a seat in the coffee shop. "Sit there." She looked up at Teddy. "Call Harvey," she said quietly, Teddy nodded and walked to the far corner of the shop to make the call.

The coffee shop door slammed open, and Sully came running in. "What the hell happened?" he asked, looking around at the concerned faces. His eyes settled on Alex who was sitting with her entire body folded in on itself as she sobbed. He moved immediately to her and took her into his arms. "It's going to be okay," he soothed. He looked up towards Teddy and Lou. "What's happened?" he asked, his tone coated with fear.

∞ ∞ ∞

Harvey Mack was a man used to dealing with intimidating women. He had been married to Marion Mack for almost fifteen years; a feat that meant he deserved a medal pinned to his chest rather than the Deputy Sheriff's badge that was currently there. However, dealing with a distraught mother was a whole different ball of wax, and he couldn't help but feel that anything he said or did was going to result in Alex tearing his head off.

"Harvey, why don't you just come out and ask us straight?" Alex said angrily. "She hasn't run away 'cause she was in trouble, she was seen getting in a car. What are you doing about that?"

They had moved to Alex's home and were sitting in the living room perched on various seats. The room was filled with an almost visceral tension.

The tall Deputy Sheriff stood awkwardly looking down at the distraught family. He chewed on his bottom lip. "We have a State-wide Amber Alert out. I have to ask these questions, Alex. I'm not questioning your's or Sully's parenting skills. We all know how much you love Jessica."

Alex closed her eyes tightly. "I'm sorry, I..." she trailed off, her brain was unable to function sufficiently to create the words. She looked down at her lap where her fingers were absently shredding a tissue. Her feet were surrounded by what looked like large snowflakes.

"So take me back through the last forty-eight hours. Was there anything unusual?" Harvey asked, he held up a finger to halt their response as his phone vibrated. "Hello?" he answered, leaving the living room to get some privacy. "When? And they have the proof?" He took in a deep breath. "Okay, get someone over there to check out what they've got and speak to the driver." He hung the phone up and turned back into the room. "They've managed to trace the car from the full description Jessica's friend gave us. It's from a town car hire company in St Anton." He took a deep breath. "They had a booking in your name, Alex, paid for by credit card and all done via email."

Alex's face crumpled in confusion. "But I never..." she paused. "Where did the car take her?"

"The airport."

∞ ∞ ∞

Maddie leaned forward to punch the call button on the elevator. She stood up straight and pulled her leather jacket tighter around her body. It had been a long shift, and all she wanted to do was crawl into her bed and sleep for a week.

"Doctor Marinelli!"

Turning her tired eyes to where her name was being called from, Maddie allowed her head to slump as the nurse waved a phone receiver towards her. She held her hands up and waved them mouthing 'No' to the nurse.

"It's the airport, Doctor Marinelli. Your niece is there. You were supposed to collect her!" the nurse replied, giving Maddie a look of disgust that she had forgotten to do something so important.

"My niece?" Maddie repeated confused. She walked back towards the nurses' station. "I...what?" she said to herself as she reached out for the phone. "Hi, Doctor Maddie Marinelli."

An unimpressed voice reached Maddie's ears. "Doctor Marinelli, this is San Francisco airport. We have your niece Jessica Milne-Sullivan here awaiting your collection. Doctor Marinelli? Doctor Marinelli, are you there?"

The nurse picked the phone up from where Maddie had slammed it down on the counter and watched as the doctor yanked open the door to the stairwell. "She's on her way now," the nurse said sweetly into the receiver and hung the phone up.

"Zoe!" Maddie yelled as she spotted her friend about to leave the hospital.

Zoe looked up from her phone. "Oh hey, I was just texting you. Mitchell's coming over tonight, hope that's okay? I was going to order pizza. Do you want to share?"

Maddie shook her head, unable to speak as she tried to get her breath back from running down five flights of stairs. "Did you drive in this morning?" she gasped.

"Yeah, I...oww, you're pinching me," Zoe complained, as Maddie grabbed her arm and propelled her through the hospital entrance.

"Excellent, you need to drive me to the airport," Maddie said, scanning the parking lot for Zoe's car. Spotting it, she dragged her friend towards it.

Running to keep up with Maddie's strides Zoe's free hand dug around in her pocket for her car keys. "Have you changed your mind again and decided to go back to Hicksville?" she asked, as Maddie spun her towards her car and let go.

"No, I have an unexpected visitor," she replied, waiting on Zoe to press her key fob to open the door. She slipped into the passenger seat and pulled out her phone, selecting the only number from Grace Falls that she had stored.

∞ ∞ ∞

Mack was grumbling to herself as she picked up her son Lewis' toys from the floor and tossed them towards his toy box. An unfamiliar ring caught her attention, initially thinking it was a toy she ignored it until its persistence won her over and she located it. She looked in surprise as she tracked the noise down to the clinic's ancient cell phone that Maddie had returned.

"Hello?" her eyes opened wider as she listened to the voice on the other end.

∞ ∞ ∞

"What do you mean they took her to the airport. How did?" Alex started to ask, pausing as her house phone rang. Teddy held her hand up to show that she was getting it.

Another officer entered the room. He caught Harvey's attention and jerked his head towards the hallway. "Harvey."

"Excuse me," Harvey said, following his colleague out.

Teddy picked up the handset and listened. "Oh thank God. She's there, and she's okay?" she asked, feeling tears of relief starting to brim in her eyes. She put her hand over the phone. "It's Mack. Jessica's in San Francisco." She watched for her friend's reaction to the next piece of information. "With Maddie."

"What?" Alex and Sully asked simultaneously.

"Hang on, I need a pen," Teddy spoke into the phone, looking around for something to write with. She rummaged through a drawer until she found a pen and scribbled the number Mack was giving her onto a scrap of paper. "Okay, got it. Thanks for calling, Mack. Yeah, we are too." She smiled hanging up. "Maddie got a call at work to go get her at the airport."

Alex flopped down onto a chair. Her relief at knowing her child was safe was palpable as she sat exhaling softly.

Harvey re-entered with his colleague. "Douglas here has spoken to the driver of the hire company. She got on a flight to San Francisco."

"We know," Teddy responded. "We just got a call. She's flown out to see the doc who was here a couple of weeks ago."

"The one with the broken down car?" Douglas asked with a look of confusion. "Well at least we know she's safe." He smiled towards Teddy.

"She is until I get my hands on her," Alex growled ominously. "I'm going to kill her."

Sully laid a hand on Alex's shoulder. "I don't get how this could have happened."

"The driver said she had the consent form signed and he just waited with her until the airline took her on as an unaccompanied minor," Douglas replied.

"But she must've done all this on the internet, and we're careful with her ever since the pony incident," Sully said, running a hand through his hair.

Alex looked up. "The computer has a password on it. I don't get it either."

Teddy looked over at her friend. "Milne1974?" she asked.

"Yeah, how did you know that?" Alex screwed her face up in confusion. "I've never told you that."

"You didn't have to, you're that predictable Alex," Teddy replied. "Looks like she's graduated from buying horses on e-bay. We know she's bright that's why we have her on the Talented and Gifted program at school!"

Sully couldn't help the small, proud smile on his lips. "Our daughter is one smart cookie," he said, shrugging as Alex glared at him. "What! She is. She's going to end up as president or something."

"Jail is where she'll end up, for computer hacking and credit card fraud," Alex countered. She stood up and lifted the laptop up from the table. "Guess we'd better get some flights booked to go get her back."

∞ ∞ ∞

Maddie and Zoe entered the arrivals hall looking around for the service desk. Spotting the sign, Maddie practically ran towards it. "Hi, I'm here to collect a child," she said quickly.

"You make it sound like you just bought her!" Zoe said as she arrived behind Maddie. Her head jerked back as she caught sight of the glare Maddie fired in her direction. "Woah, someone's snarky."

"Jessica Milne-Sullivan. I got a call," Maddie said turning back to the woman behind the desk and flashing an apologetic smile.

Recognizing the name, the woman narrowed her eyes at Maddie. "The child you were meant to pick up over an hour ago?" she said. "Can I see some ID?"

Maddie pulled out her driver's license and slipped it over the desk. The woman checked it and pulled up the details on the computer. "Okay." She passed back the ID and picked up a phone. "Hey, Mandy, someone is here for Jessica. Can you bring her down?" Her friendly tone and smile immediately disappeared as she put the phone down and looked at Maddie again. "She'll be a minute."

Maddie paced back and forth as Zoe browsed the tourist leaflets. "You know I should probably go check out Alcatraz at some point," Zoe remarked, turning a leaflet around in her hand.

"Maddie-Lyn!"

Maddie spun around to where Jessica was being escorted by an airline worker in uniform. The young girl was tugging at the woman's hand to make her go faster to get to Maddie. Finally, when she was close enough, she broke free and ran the distance to Maddie, her backpack bouncing up and down as she ran. She reached Maddie and gripped her around her waist. Maddie looked at the airline worker. "Thank you," she said, getting a stony stare in reply.

"Yeah, you're never gonna get an upgrade here," Zoe remarked, putting the leaflet back and watching as the airline worker gave Maddie a final look up and down before leaving them.

"Jessica, what are you doing here?" Maddie asked staring down at the child hugging her.

Jessica looked up, her blue eyes were open wide. "You never said goodbye, and you promised to draw with me and name all the bones...and I tried. I've been drawing skeletons, but they don't look right, and Aunt Teddy was rubbish at naming the bones, even though she said she'd help me, 'cause you couldn't since you'd gone, but not gone like my Uncle Bear 'cause he's dead, and you're just gone." She let the last bit of air in her lungs gush out. "Have you called my mama?" she asked, her tone tinged with worry.

"I called Mack to get her to tell your mommy that you're okay," Maddie answered, pulling Jessica into a hug. "I think there's probably been a lot of worried people back at Grace Falls. How did you? I mean, just how?"

Jessica shrugged. "I booked a flight using my mama's credit card, and then I booked a car to take me to the airport and emailed them using my mama's email." She squinted as she remembered all the steps she had taken to get there. "I had to print off the permission slip from the airline. So I switched off mama's alarm and got her super late so she wouldn't see what she was signing and told her it was for a trip, and got her to sign it."

Maddie and Zoe's eyes widened in amazement as they listened to Jessica taking them through her deception in a matter of fact manner listing off her actions against her fingers.

"And then I was staying at my daddy's overnight. So I used his phone to text Aunt Teddy to say I was ill, and wouldn't be at school."

"She's like a freaking evil genius mixed with Ferris Bueller." Zoe snorted shaking her head in astonishment.

The small girl turned her head and looked at Zoe for the first time. "I'm Jessica, who are you?"

Zoe blinked in surprise. "You're blunt and to the point. I like you. I'm Zoe, Maddie's friend."

Jessica narrowed her eyes. "My mama's prettier than you."

"Aaaand now I don't like you!" Zoe said tilting her head to the side. "Can you send her back now?" she asked Maddie, giving her a sickly sweet smile.

"Crap," Maddie said. "I didn't even think about how we get you back. Umm." She looked around suddenly panicked that she would have to take Jessica back to Grace Falls herself. She was still running through the possibilities when her phone rang. "Hi." Her voice faltered slightly as the thought that it could be Alex struck her.

"Maddie, it's Sully. Is Jessica there with you? Can I speak to her?"

"Sure." Maddie handed the cell over to Jessica. "It's your daddy."

The young girl took the cell phone in both hands. "Hi."

"Jessica? Are you okay?" Despite knowing that his daughter was safe, Sully was still filled with trepidation until he heard Jessica's voice.

"Yes," Jessica answered. "Are you and mama very mad at me?"

"You remember what it was like with the pony?" Sully asked. "Well multiply that by around a thousand." He sighed not wanting to scare Jessica too much. "But we're just mad 'cause we were so worried that we'd lost you and because apparently, you chose an expensive flight to put on Mama's credit card," he added, waving his hand to shush Alex as she pitched in behind him. "We love you very much."

"I'm sorry I worried everyone, but I wanted to draw skeletons with Maddie like she promised."

Sully sighed. "I know, sport. Can you put Maddie back on for me?"

Jessica handed the phone back to Maddie. "I'm in biiig trouble," she said, pulling her mouth into a frown.

"Hey, Maddie," Sully said. His voice was laced with tiredness following the emotionally draining afternoon they'd had. "We're going to fly out, but we can't get a flight until tomorrow morning. Can Jessica stay with you tonight?"

Maddie swallowed, looking between Jessica and Zoe who was regarding the child through narrowed eyes. "Sure. What time does your flight get in tomorrow? I'll bring her to the airport." Zoe rolled her eyes as Maddie listened to the flight details. "Okay, see you tomorrow." She looked down at Jessica. "Well, we'll have plenty time to draw skeletons tonight. You're staying with us." She put her hands on Jessica's shoulders and started to march her towards the exit as she mouthed an apology to Zoe.

∞ ∞ ∞

"What's that one called?" Jessica asked with one finger pointing towards a diagram as her other hand tried to negotiate a slice of pizza into her mouth.

Maddie leaned forward on the sofa to look at where she was pointing. "Fibula," she confirmed, before beating Zoe to the final slice of pizza and earning a scowl from her friend.

"You should get to know the heart kiddo, much cooler than bones," Zoe said. "I'm a cardiologist, that means I know everything about hearts."

"No thanks," Jessica replied without looking up. Zoe tilted her head and jerked it furiously as she got up and walked over to the kitchen.

"Be right back," Maddie said, rubbing Jessica's back and getting up to follow Zoe.

Zoe pulled a beer out of the fridge. "The kid hates me," she whispered.

"I've no idea what's going on with her, I'm sorry," Maddie said, watching Jessica as the young girl studied the books that Maddie had brought out for her.

"So that's Alex's daughter."

Maddie pulled the fridge door open and snagged a beer. She took the opener from Zoe and popped the cap off the bottle. "Yeah," she sighed wistfully.

"I still can't believe you, Maddie Marinelli, were going to choose to stay in Hicksville for love over heading up the ER in a major San Francisco hospital," Zoe said incredulously.

Slapping Zoe's arm, Maddie shushed her roommate. "Shhh, keep your voice down."

The door to the apartment opened, and Mitchell entered. "Hi, I hope you're hungry I brought..." He stopped as he spotted the blonde child kneeling beside the coffee table pouring over medical books. He shrugged one arm out of his jacket and switched the pizza box he was holding into his other hand as he let his jacket fall onto the sofa.

"Mitchell, this is Jessica. Jessica, this is Mitchell," Maddie said, moving back towards the living area of the apartment.

"Hi," Mitchell said, as Zoe kissed his cheek and took the pizza box from him towards the kitchen area.

Jessica looked at Mitchell and Zoe. "Is Zoe your girlfriend?" Jessica asked.

Huffing slightly in surprise at the question, Mitchell looked at the two other adults and Jessica before replying. "Um yes, yes she is."

The young girl broke into a wild smile, and her dimples popped in each cheek. "Zoe, can you show me the heart stuff now?"

Zoe raised her head out from inspecting the pizza that Mitchell had brought, her eyebrows raised in surprise. "Ehhh, sure," she said carefully, lifting a slice of pizza before walking over and settling herself down beside Jessica. She looked up at Maddie who shrugged in response.

∞ ∞ ∞

Maddie pulled a hoodie on over her tank top and wandered out of her bathroom. Sitting cross-legged in the center of her bed was Jessica.

"Mama has that sweatshirt," Jessica said. "Did you brush your teeth?"

"Yes I did," Maddie replied, ignoring Jessica's remark about the sweatshirt. When she had unpacked her belongings, she had found the grey sweatshirt, with a crimson A on its chest, that Alex had loaned her following her altercation with the skunk. Despite knowing she should, she was yet to return it and had instead started to wear it. "Now scoot over," she instructed, pulling the covers back for the young girl to climb in. She tucked the covers down then walked around the bed and climbed in. Laying down she switched the light on her nightstand off plunging the room into darkness.

"Do you still like my mama?" Jessica asked.

Maddie rolled her eyes. She had wanted to avoid any discussions with Jessica about the circumstances of her leaving Grace Falls. The child's interest in all things anatomy had kept her occupied through the evening meaning the subject was never raised, but now it looked like she was going to make Maddie talk.

"Yes I still like your mommy, but it's complicated."

"Aunt Teddy says that when something is complicated you just have to break it down into its component parts, and that way it makes it much simpler," Jessica said, wriggling down underneath the duvet.

"Well that's very sound advice," Maddie said, her lips twitching into a smirk at Jessica's advice. "I'll be sure to consider that, now sleep," she said mustering up an authoritarian tone.

"Maybe if you told me the component parts I could work it out. I'm pretty clever for my age."

Maddie let out a soft laugh. "I know that. You being here is proof of how clever you are, but you really can't help with this one, sweetie. So sleep." Maddie closed her eyes and felt herself start to drift off. The last thing she heard before she fell asleep was Jessica's voice.

"My mama still likes you too."

Chapter Twelve

"She gets it from you, you know," Alex grumped, nodding her acknowledgment to the air steward who was preparing the cabin for landing. She pushed the window blind up complying with the steward's request and winced as the bright sunlight shone through the small window of the plane.

Sully turned in his seat. "The smartness. Really? You think?"

"The sneakiness," Alex clarified. "The smartness comes from me." Her right leg jiggled up and down with nerves. The closer they got to San Francisco the more Alex started to think about what she wanted to say to Maddie. She could feel the pent-up frustration coursing through her as her mind created various scenarios on what their meeting would be like. Sully reached over and placed his hand on her knee stalling her movement.

"Wanna talk about it?" he asked.

Alex rolled her eyes and allowed her head to flop back against the headrest. "I'm nervous about seeing Madeleine again. I don't know whether I want to smack her or kiss her."

"Go for both, in that order," Sully said, furrowing his brow and looking serious.

"You're not helping," Alex groaned, rolling her head to the side to look at her now grinning friend.

Sully laughed and squeezed her knee. "You were mad because she didn't let you defend yourself, so now you can."

"I wish I was just mad. I'm hurt Matt. She hurt me. I haven't opened myself up to anyone in years and then I do and..." She huffed and looked back at the console above her head. "Being mad is easy, but mostly when I think about her, I'm sad. Sad that I misjudged who I thought she was. Sad that I allowed myself to think that I could have the happy ending with her." She raised her hand and wiped angrily at the tear that was tracing its way down the side of her face. Sully leaned over and pressed his lips against the side of her head before he rested his head against hers.

"You should tell her that then," he said softly.

∞ ∞ ∞

Sully followed the exit signs through the arrivals area. "She said she'd get us at the customer service desk," he said, looking around. He turned to speak to Alex before realizing that she was no longer by his side. He spun around seeing her standing ten yards behind him. He frowned and retraced his steps. "She'll be at the customer service desk."

"I don't think I can," Alex said, shaking her head.

"Don't think you can what?"

Alex shook her hands as if trying to loosen the tension from her body. "Ugh." She looked up at the ceiling attempting to tip the tears that were welling in her eyes back in. "God," she groaned, giving up and wiping her eyes. "I don't know what to say, Matt. I...I...it hurts." She balled her hand into a fist and held it to her chest.

Sully stepped closer to her and wrapped his arms around her. "The stuff that matters usually does."

∞ ∞ ∞

Maddie stood at the customer service desk. She held onto Jessica's hand as she scanned the arrivals board. "Their flight has landed," she said, managing to sound brighter and less nervous than she felt. Her stomach had started to churn from the moment she had woken up at the thought of seeing Alex again. She had been unable to eat anything for breakfast. Since then her nervousness had reached a level she had not experienced since sitting her finals. Maddie was torn between wanting to see Alex again and not wanting another visual reminder of how she had mistaken their mutual attraction for anything deeper than that. She still felt the burn of the humiliation of being lied to and called 'easy.' However, the part of her that refused to return the borrowed sweatshirt had to admit to still wanting her. As she tried to sort through her emotions, she felt a tug on her hand.

"Daddy!" Jessica exclaimed, releasing Maddie's hand and running towards Sully who was standing with his arms outstretched.

He scooped his daughter up into a tight hug, peppering her face with kisses. "Do. Not. Ever. Do. That. Again," he said, walking them towards Maddie.

"I won't, I promise," Jessica said, wrapping her arms around his neck. "Where's Mama," she asked, twisting so she could look past her father's head.

"She's waiting inside," Sully said, watching Maddie's face and seeing a look that was a mix of disappointment and relief flash across her features. "Maddie, thank you for looking after her," he said, adjusting his hold on Jessica and holding out his hand.

Maddie shook it. "No problem. I'm sorry if anything I said contributed to this."

He shook his head. "No, this is all on Jessica," he replied, looking sidelong at his daughter. "Thanks again." He took Jessica's backpack from Maddie and turned to leave. He took two paces then stopped and turned back again, "She didn't know about Sam and Peter's plan. They didn't tell her as she would have told you. She's the most honest person I know." Maddie opened her mouth, but Sully held his hand up to stop her, the backpack dangling from it. "And the bet. We bet on everything. We bet because it reminds us of Alex's brother who is no longer with us and who loved to bet on stupid things. We all do it. Except for Alex. She's never bet on anything in her life. The only thing she took a gamble on was you." He looked sadly at Maddie. "And it looks like she lost that one." He gave a nod, satisfied that if Alex was unable to defend herself then at least he had. Not waiting for a response he turned to leave.

"She called me easy," Maddie yelled after him.

Sully turned around again. "You one hundred percent sure on that? 'cause by my reckoning, you're two for two on being wrong so far." He looked at Jessica. "Say bye to Doctor Marinelli, Jessica."

"Bye, Maddie-Lyn," Jessica said, waving her hand. "Thank you for my skeletons. Say bye to Zoe for me."

Sully turned and walked back towards security with Jessica bouncing up and down in his arms as she waved to Maddie.

Maddie waved until they disappeared around a corner. Her hand then dropped to her side, and she gulped in air as she processed Sully's words. She realized that right now, she wasn't sure about a damn thing anymore.

∞ ∞ ∞

"Can I have a story?" Jessica asked. Her eyes were wide with innocence as she tried to convince her mother.

Alex bit her lip. Her ability to stay mad at her daughter was always sorely tested when she gave her the puppy dog look. "Do you really think you should be asking for that after your adventures?" she said, managing to coax out a half decent attempt at seriousness.

Jessica pouted. "No...I'm sorry I worried you all."

Leaning down, Alex kissed her daughter's head. "Yeah, well you're still grounded 'til you're thirty and no computer ever," she said against her daughter's hair. She stood up straight and turned the light off. "Night night." Alex rested her hand on the doorframe and gave her daughter one last look. She had almost closed the door when Jessica tried one last ploy to stay up.

"Mama, where's Hicksville?"

Alex opened the door again. "Where did you hear that?"

"Zoe said it to Maddie-Lyn. She said that Maddie-Lyn almost chose love and stayed in Hicksville. Where is it? Can we go?"

Alex's mouth opened as she took in what Jessica had said. She stood with her mouth gaping open and an inability to process what her daughter was telling her; her thoughts were disrupted as Jessica pursued her question.

"Mama, are you listening to me? Can we go there?"

Shaking her head to clear it Alex closed her eyes and took in a breath. "It's nowhere, sweetie, Zoe or whatever her name was must have got it wrong." She turned and stepped out of Jessica's room.

"No I definitely heard her say Hicksville," the young girl called after her mother.

"Sleep Jessica," Alex called, waking down in the hallway in a daze. She pulled out her cell and selected Teddy's name, and typed a text. '*Need you...bring Jack!*'

∞ ∞ ∞

"Hey, sorry I'm late, you will not believe where I've been." Teddy dropped her jacket over the stair handrail and poked her head into the downstairs rooms as she walked through the house looking for Alex. "Remember that Deputy that was here yesterday. Not Harvey, the other one; Douglas. He asked me out." She paused, frowning, as she entered the kitchen and found it empty. She noticed the empty bottle of Jim Beam on the table. "Looks like Jim got here first Jack," she said lifting up the bottle of Jack Daniels in her hand and speaking to it. "Alex?" she called. When she didn't get a response, she headed out towards the back porch, fully expecting to see Alex on the swing. Finding it vacant, her concern increased.

"Marco!" she yelled, putting the bottle of Jack Daniels down onto the swing and looking out into the darkness of the garden. She heard a faint 'Polo' coming from near the bottom of the garden. Stepping forward Teddy spotted where it was coming from. "Awwwww crap," she muttered, digging her cell from her pocket. "Sully, it's Teddy. Can you come to Alex's?" She rolled her eyes as Sully started to protest. "Yes, I know it's a Friday, but she's gone on a Bear hunt. Yeah, you heard right." She hung up and started to make her way down the garden, muttering curses as she went.

∞ ∞ ∞

Sully looked up. "Well, how in the hell did she get up there!"

Teddy stood beside him with her arms crossed tight against her chest. "How does she always get up there? She climbed."

They looked up into the tall tree that sat at the bottom of Alex's garden. Halfway up its stout trunk a small wooden platform had been built. From their position on the ground, they could see the lower parts of Alex's legs dangling from it. "I swear to God I'm going to tear that down," Sully growled standing on his tiptoes to get a better look.

"You said that the last time," Teddy remarked, "and the time before that." A small smile started to play on her lips. "And I'm pretty sure that you said that the day that Bear built it and we got stuck up there."

"And I meant it," Sully said, looking sideways at Teddy.

"Just do what you always do. Go get her." Teddy waved up towards the platform.

Sully blew out a long breath. "I haven't done that in years. I'm not as young as I used to be...and...and she's had a kid since the last time I carried her down," he said quietly.

Teddy snorted. "I'm so telling her you said that when she's sober."

Ignoring her Sully looked back to the trailing feet. "So do we know why she's sunk a bottle of JB and climbed Bear's tree?"

Teddy shook her head and shrugged. "Nope, I got a text from her earlier asking me to come over but I was running late, and she was up there when I arrived. How did things go in San Francisco?"

Sully gave a small huff. "Let's not go there. So how was your date?"

Teddy turned to look at him her mouth open in shock. "How?" her eyes narrowed. "Lou. I'll kill her," she murmured. "It was very nice thank you."

"I could be dead up here you know," a slurred voice announced above them.

"Are you?" Sully asked.

"Nooooo," Alex replied.

"Teddy had a date," he shouted, getting a slap on the arm from Teddy. Alex sat up and blinked trying to clear her vision, then looked down at her friends.

"You did?" she grinned. "Thasss great!" Her smile faded quickly. "Love sucks." She flopped backward, her legs lifting with the momentum.

"Honey, you're going to have to come down," Teddy said, tipping her head back.

"Donwanna."

Teddy and Sully exchanged frustrated looks.

"Daddy?" A tired voice came from behind them. They turned towards the house. Standing in her nightdress rubbing her eyes with a balled fist stood Jessica. Her tiredness making her look younger than her years.

"I got this," Teddy said. "Hey, fugitive," she grinned jogging back towards the porch and scooping Jessica up. "C'mon I'll take you back upstairs." She carried the girl back into the house leaving Sully with Alex.

Sully watched Teddy disappear, then turned his attention back towards the feet dangling above his head.

"She was gonna stay, Matt."

He dropped his head and kicked the toe of his shoe against the ground. "You don't know that for sure."

"I do, Jessicatolme," she garbled, sitting upright again before swaying slightly back and forth.

"Jessica's seven. What does she know? Apart from how to hack a computer and lie and cheat her way across half the country." His eyes pleaded with Alex. "Please come down."

"I can't."

"Please!"

Alex closed her eyes and shook her head. The action took her dangerously close to coming out of the tree quicker than either of them were ready for. "No. I actually can't, Matt. I tried, but I'm too drunk to get back down."

Sully looked up into the night sky. "Bear, if you weren't already dead, I'd kill you for building that damn thing." He stepped forward and took hold of Alex's ankles. "Okay lean forward and try to lower yourself slowly."

Alex scooted forward and balanced her weight on her hands. She moved her backside off the platform, feeling Sully's strong arms around her legs as he guided her down. She felt the muscles in her arms start to shake at the exertion and gasped as they gave out, speeding her descent. Sully let out an 'Oomph' as Alex's upper body landed on his shoulder and he struggled to keep his knees from giving out at the impact. Standing up straight, he kept Alex in a fireman's lift and started back up towards the house.

Bouncing up and down, with her face almost level with Sully's ass, she spotted his cell phone in the back pocket of his jeans. She pulled the cell out and selected a number from his recent calls list.

Sully was climbing the steps of the porch when he heard Alex's voice.

"Hmmm voicemail, well that doesssn't surprise me since you left me! You freakin' left me standing in the middle of the road! This might of just been a fling for you, Madeleine. A woman in every port as you swing on by, but I'm worth more than that and I just wanted to tell you that you're a coward. Yep, thas right a coward."

Sully's eyes widened in horror as he realized he no longer felt the weight of his cell phone in his pocket. He used his spare hand to try and grab the phone from Alex before she made it worse, but she slapped his hand away furiously as she continued to leave her message.

"Jessica said you were going to stay, but I guess you got scared, and you ran, and you can try and blame me but I...I didn' do anyfin.' This was you." The anger started to disappear from her voice. "And I'm a coward, 'cause I couldn't face seeing you today. When all I really wanted was to see you. Just so you know, I don't want to sleep with you." She hung the call up and allowed Sully's grasping hand to snatch the phone from her. As he carried her through the kitchen, she felt a tightness in her chest as if someone was pushing their hand against it. She started to gulp in air. Her breathing increased as her inverted position, and the movement of Sully's strides started to make her feel nauseous.

"Do not barf on meeeaaaawww crap, Alex." Sully sighed, exasperated at the feeling of hot liquid hitting the back of his legs.

∞ ∞ ∞

Maddie rubbed her eyes. Thanks to a changed shift to accommodate Jessica's unscheduled visit, and a freeway pile up, it was now two in the morning. She had been at the hospital since she had handed Jessica over to Sully the previous morning. She yawned and picked up the chart of a patient that she wanted to follow up on before leaving. Since her experience in Grace Falls, she had found that more, and more, she was less satisfied with just treating emergencies. Often her curiosity had her tracking down patients that she had seen to find out what happened to them. She scanned the notes jotted in by her interns as she walked towards the room. She was surprised to see the man sitting up in bed. The glow from the TV set positioned on the wall was reflecting on his face.

"Hey, Mr. Lewis what you doing up?" she asked. "Are you in pain?" She looked down the chart to see the dosage of pain medication he was on.

"Nah, just can't sleep." he smiled. "You checking up on me again, Dr. Marinelli?"

"What can I say? I like to keep tabs on the people I like!" Maddie grinned. Satisfied that he was okay, she turned to exit the room and return the chart before Mr. Lewis' voice stopped her at the door.

"You have to admire his tenacity?"

Maddie turned back and frowned. "Whose?"

The old man indicated towards the TV with his head. Maddie stepped further into the room to see the TV screen. "You're watching cartoons in the middle of the night?"

"This is not just a cartoon; this is Loony Tunes."

Maddie laughed. "So whose tenacity do I have to admire?" She looked up at the screen.

"Pepe Le Pew," he said. "Every time he thinks he's struck gold, only to find out that it's a cat with white paint down her back and yet every time she runs away he just skips on behind, never doubting his love."

"Well as one who has been on the wrong end of a skunk, I'm with the cat," Maddie said reaching up and switching the TV off. "You should get some sleep." She stepped out of the room and closed the door behind her. Leaning on it she bit her top lip remembering with a smile the incident and what it led to. Her smile faded as she thought about how Alex couldn't even bring herself to see her at the airport.

She put the patient file back into the slot on the nurse's station and walked towards the resident's lounge to change before leaving.

"Hey, you?"

Maddie smiled at Zoe rubbing at the soles of her feet. "You know if you wore sensible shoes your feet wouldn't ache."

"Yeah, but my heart would," Zoe replied.

Maddie snorted as she checked her cell phone. She spotted the symbol for a voicemail and dialed the number to retrieve it.

Zoe watched as Maddie listened to her cell, her hand reached up to press against her locker for support while keeping her back towards her friend. Maddie hung up the call and stood, her head bowed.

"You okay?" Zoe asked concerned.

Maddie turned around. Her eyes were bright with unshed tears. "Yeah, I'm good."

Sensing the need for a change of subject Zoe slapped her thighs and stood up. "I'm surprised to still see you here."

Maddie nodded slowly. "Yeah, you know what, I shouldn't be here." She flashed Zoe a small smile and grabbed her leather jacket from the locker and walked quickly towards the door.

∞ ∞ ∞

Alex woke slowly. Her eyes felt as though they had been glued closed. Her tongue was welded to the roof of her mouth, and a dull pain pounded rhythmically behind her right eye. She shifted slowly opening one eye to inspect the weight she could feel on her chest. Her vision took a moment to adjust, and it took a tad longer before her brain was able to process the image and make sense of it. Slung across her breasts was a man's arm. She frowned and slowly rolled her open eye to the side. Her right eye remained firmly closed. She raised an eyebrow at the sight of Sully sleeping beside her. His nose twitched as he slept. She went to speak, immediately remembering the dryness of her mouth. She winced as she swallowed, trying to muster up some saliva.

"Matt?" she croaked.

Still asleep Sully moaned at the sound of his name piercing his consciousness. Alex lifted the arm that wasn't pinned under Sully's and slapped his forearm. "Matt!"

He jumped slightly as his eyes sprung open.

"What?" he groaned.

"Why are you in my bed?" Alex asked, turning her head carefully towards him and attempting to open her right eye; immediately regretting it and snapping it closed again.

Sully lifted the arm that rested across Alex and started to trace his fingers across her neck. "You mean you don't remember?" he asked. His eyebrows furrowed and a look of hurt appeared in his eyes. "I asked whether you were sure and you said yes. I knew it was a mistake," he said sighing, "but you wanted it so badly." He withdrew his hand and pulled the duvet up around himself. "You wanted us to make a little brother or sister for Jessica. Please tell me you remember."

Alex looked at him in horror, her mouth gaped open, and she sat bolt upright. She wobbled slightly as her balance struggled to keep up with her movement. "I...I..." she stammered. She stopped and narrowed her eyes as she pulled the duvet away from her body. "I'm fully clothed," she said evenly, turning to glare at a now grinning Sully.

"You barfed over my jeans, now we're even." Sully laughed. "You were so out of it. I didn't want to leave you. As much as I love our daughter, I don't want to be a single parent."

Alex flipped the duvet off her and swung her legs out of bed.

"Oh my God he got to you too," Teddy said from the doorway, with a cup of steaming coffee in her hand, and a smirk on her face as she teased her friend.

Alex strode over, snatched the mug from Teddy, and took a sip. "You're my friend, how come I didn't wake up beside you instead of morning glory over there?"

Sully shifted the covers over himself. "It's not my fault, it just happens," he murmured. He nodded his head towards Teddy. "She did stay. By the time I got you upstairs she was passed out beside Jessica."

"Sorry!" Teddy said taking the mug back from Alex and drinking. "I was more tired than I thought."

"Dates'll do that to you," Sully said, locking his arms behind his head.

Alex swiveled around to look at Teddy. "You had a date? Who with?"

"Hey, Mama, why were you up the tree?" Jessica asked, entering the room and rubbing her eyes. She did a double take at her father lying sprawled across her mother's bed. "Daddy?" she smiled and launched herself towards the bed. "Is Aunt Lou here too?"

"Just when you think things couldn't get weirder," Alex mumbled under her breath.

Teddy snorted at the comment.

"Was I up Bear's tree?" Alex asked, looking at Sully, tickling Jessica on the bed, and Teddy sipping her coffee in the doorway.

Sully stopped tickling Jessica for a moment and looked at Alex. "You don't remember?" he asked. "Anything?"

Running a hand through her hair and wondering how much she had drunk to make even that a painful experience, Alex shook her head carefully. "No, I really don't."

"Jessica, why don't you go get washed up," Sully said guiding his daughter towards the edge of the bed. "Now!" he said, spotting the look in his daughter's face that telegraphed that she was about to object. The young girl pouted but scooted off the bed and skipped back out of the room.

"What did I do?" Alex said feeling worried at the serious look on Sully's face. She turned to Teddy who brought her shoulders up to her ears and shrugged.

Sully pulled himself up and lifted his legs over the side of the bed, gripping the edge of the mattress at either side of his thighs. "You may or may not have drunk-dialed Maddie," he said bobbing his head back and forth as he spoke.

"I may not have?" Alex asked hopefully. Her eyebrows rose up so far that they almost touched her hairline.

Sully pursed his lips. "No, you definitely did." He gave her a tight smile. "I tried to stop you, but you're strong when you want to be."

Alex fell back until her back rested against the door. "I've made it worse, haven't I?" she moaned.

"You know I think you might have," he replied grimacing on Alex's behalf. "I mean it was bad enough she thinks you called her easy, but now you actually called her a coward." He held his hands up and pursed his lips.

"What? I never called her easy," Alex spluttered, she spun around. All traces of her hangover were momentarily forgotten. "What *exactly* did you say in that bathroom, Claudia Roosevelt?"

Teddy recoiled at the use of her full name. "We spoke about the car, and the bet, then Lou said something about how long it took for you two to hook up, and I joked that you had complained...oh God"—Teddy's eyes widened—"I'm sorry Alex. I said something about us thinking you were easy, she must have thought I meant her. I'm sorry, I'll call her. I'll tell her now," Teddy said, clutching Alex's hand.

Alex closed her eyes and bit her bottom lip a distant memory was tugging persistently at her brain. "Sully, what else did I say on the call last night?"

"That you were worth more and she was a coward. I'm kinda paraphrasing here," he said apologetically. "I was too busy trying to get the phone off you to listen fully. Oh, and you told her, for her information, that you didn't want to sleep with her. Which, I have to say, I flinched at."

Alex's breath caught, and she walked off into her bathroom and closed the door softly behind her. Sully looked at Teddy in confusion. "What the hell just...?" He lifted his hand and pointed towards the door.

Teddy gave an imperceptible shake of her head. "In Alex speak, she drunkenly told Maddie she loved her." She sighed as she watched the closed door.

Sully frowned. "Just when I think I'm getting the hang of women, you change the rules, and I'm as confused as ever." He stood up and rubbed the back of his head. "You know I reckon the only thing more complicated than being in a relationship with a woman is being a woman in a relationship with a woman."

Glancing over towards him Teddy frowned. "Put some damn pants on."

Chapter Thirteen

One week later...

Lou leaned on the counter resting her chin in her hands as she watched the rain bounce off the sidewalk outside. "I'm fed up of this rain now." She puffed as she twisted her head to look over at Alex who was seated at one of the tables in the empty coffee shop. Her feet were resting on a chair as she completed a crossword puzzle nestled on her lap.

"It's been raining for twenty minutes, Lou. It's hardly monsoon season," Alex murmured, not taking her eyes from the crossword as she reached for her half-empty coffee cup.

Huffing, Lou turned and pulled herself up to sit on the counter. She picked up a plastic spoon and started to toy with it as she contemplated saying what was on her mind."Say it. Whatever that brain of yours is struggling with, just say it," Alex said, finally putting her pen down on top of the folded newspaper and looking up at Lou. "C'mon, get it off your chest." She twirled her hand to encourage Lou to spill.

"Idon'tgetwhyyoudidn'tcallheragain," Lou gushed, her shoulders slumping at the relief at finally saying what had been pestering her for a week since Sully had told her of the drunken voicemail incident.

Alex gave a sad smile. "She never called me either, Lou."

"I know, but you two seemed so"—Lou held a deep breath as she decided on the words to use—"made for each other." She exhaled, throwing her hands up in exasperation.

"I know that you're desperate for a happy ending, Lou, but this is reality. She wasn't honestly going to give up her career and move here to be with me after only a week of knowing me." Alex looked back at her crossword, not focusing on it. She had picked the phone up a half dozen times during the week and had even dialed the number that she'd found on the notepad where Teddy had written it down. But each time she had placed the phone back down, unable to go through with it. She didn't know what else to say. She still couldn't believe that she'd called her in the first place. She was sure that after receiving the drunken call Maddie wouldn't want to hear anything she had to say ever again. She wanted so badly to rewind to when she was mad with Maddie. Being mad at oneself was turning out to be so much more work.

The bell dinged as the door to the coffee shop opened, and the sound of the rain pounding against the ground increased. Mack entered the shop and shook herself, getting rid of the excess water that clung to her jacket. "'s wild out there," she said smiling.

Lou slipped off the counter and turned ready to serve. "Hey, Mack, how's things?"

Still flicking her wrists to shake the water from her hands Mack walked towards the counter. "How's things? I'll tell you how things are. I have been a nurse for over ten years. I have brought babies into this world and held peoples' hands as they've left it. I have cleaned up the puke, shit, and snot of most of this town and now"—she pulled herself up to full height—"and now I'm working for a doctor who seems to think I am their God-dammed PA. That's how things are!" she finished, fixing Lou with a glare.

Alex licked her lips pulling her bottom lip into her mouth to stop from laughing aloud as Mack had worked herself up to a full-scale rant.

"There I am minding my own, and this over-educated, over-opinionated, impulsive, and stubborn as a mule MD decides that I, Marion Mack, should, and I quote, 'run and go get the coffees'." She looked over towards Alex who was still looking fixedly at her crossword. "You hearing me, Milne. Me!"

Alex looked up her eyes wide. "That's disgusting, Mack. I have no other words," she said managing to keep her face straight. She looked back down at her crossword, before stealing a quick glance back up towards the small nurse.

"Why would a doc send you all the way from St Anton to he—" Lou stopped as Mack shook her head.

Mack narrowed her eyes. "Hmmm. Anyways, I'll have my usual and the Doc...well, wait 'til I get this right now. She wanted a regular skinny Americano with an extra shot to go, and she wanted it in this." Mack pulled out the orange tippy cup and placed it on the counter.

Alex looked up as she heard Lou gasp. Seeing the orange cup on the counter, she lifted her legs from the chair, stood up, and walked towards the counter. Speechless, she picked it up and looked open-mouthed from the cup towards Mack.

"She's at the clinic." Mack smiled.

Alex's surprised expression turned into one of joy as she registered what Mack had said. Using her hand to propel herself from the counter and towards the door, she slammed it open and ran out into the pouring rain still holding the cup.

Mack and Lou watched her go. As the door closed, Mack held out an open palm over her shoulder.

"Really!" Lou said, digging into her pockets before scowling as she slammed a ten-dollar bill into Mack's waiting hand. "I can't believe it took her a week to come to her senses."

Mack smiled to herself. She had absolutely no intention of telling Lou that Maddie had come to her senses as soon as she'd heard Alex's call. It had just taken a week to get things lined up for her to return. She folded the bill neatly and turned to look at the younger woman. "I don't see my coffee, Anderson, and I need a cup!"

∞ ∞ ∞

Alex ran at full speed towards the clinic, ignoring the sensation of water seeping through her sneakers as she splashed through puddles. Her T-shirt and light blue shirt became stuck to her skin as the rain-soaked her. She skidded to a halt outside the white building. Standing in the doorway with a coy smile on her lips was Maddie.

"You doing door-to-door delivery on coffee these days?" she shouted, nodding towards the tippy cup in Alex's hand.

"Just for special customers," Alex yelled back, walking slowly up the pathway. Her heart was thumping in her chest. A reaction caused more by the sight of Maddie than her exertions getting to the clinic.

"So what makes a customer special?" Maddie asked, stepping down the stairs into the rain.

Alex smiled broadly. "Number one, they have to be a Grace Falls resident," she said walking up the pathway towards Maddie. She ran a hand through her wet hair, slicking it against her head.

Maddie nodded thoughtfully. "Check," she said, quirking her eyebrows. "Is there a number two?" she asked, walking down the path. The rain started to darken the blue T-shirt she was wearing.

"They have to be close to management," Alex replied. Her face pulled into a serious expression as she walked forwards.

"How close is close?" Maddie asked, strolling towards Alex until their faces were inches apart.

"Little closer," Alex said smiling.

Maddie raised her eyebrows. "This close?" She leaned closer. "I don't want to sleep with you either," she said before pressing their lips together.

Epilogue

Part One

The warm, oppressive air hit her as she opened the door. She balanced a cardboard tray with two tall cups of iced tea in one hand as she held the door open for an elderly customer. "Why young, Jessica, you get more like your mother each day." The woman smiled as she patted the young girl's shoulder.

"Which one?" Jessica asked. Momentarily, the woman looked perturbed before Jessica broke into a wide grin. "Mama, Mrs. Willis is here for ice cream," she yelled, turning her head back into the coffee shop. She leaned forward and whispered conspiratorially, "The chocolate flavor rocks." Jessica wedged the door open with her foot and turned and gave a quick wave towards her mom before stepping out into the heat that had been taunting her since she'd opened the door.

She walked along the sidewalk falling into a now practiced routine of stepping onto the cracks of the paving as she went, consciously not looking at the two filled cups. She had made this journey enough times in all seasons, and weather, to know that looking at the cups was sure to result in the contents being spilled onto her hands. She smiled as she remembered the first time that she had walked along this sidewalk flanked by her mom and Maddie. Her stride had been shorter then and punctuated with giant leaps as the two women had swung her into the air. She recalled talking nonstop to Maddie as they walked to Ben's naming ceremony. Nowadays her stride was longer, and she didn't have to almost jog to keep in step with the tall doctor. The nonstop talking, however, remained the same.

There had been a period of adjustment for all of them as Maddie settled into her new home and role. Initially, she had moved into the Anderson house before they agreed that she should move in.

Alex, for her part, took time to adjust to sharing her living space and life with someone other than her daughter. As for Jessica, she had perhaps the biggest job of all. For the first time in her life, she had to share not just her mom but also her dad, as his relationship with Lou blossomed. The adults in this rag-tag family held their breaths waiting for the enormity and unusualness of the situation to hit the child and for the inevitable fall out. However, as the weeks became months and months became years, their apprehension lessened. Unbeknown to any of them a certain nurse had made a pre-emptive strike on their behalf only a few weeks after Maddie returned to Grace Falls.

∞ ∞ ∞

Three years earlier

Mack spotted Jessica sitting on the steps of the clinic waiting for Maddie to finish. Armed with the knowledge that Maddie was still completing her now weekly checkup of Emmett Day, Mack took the opportunity to speak with the young girl. "Jessica." She smiled, pushing open the screen door and stepping out in the early evening's warmth.

"Hey, Mack." Jessica squinted up towards the woman.

"Mind if I keep you company?" Mack asked, plonking herself down before Jessica could respond. She let out a relieved sigh at finally giving her legs a rest. It had been a busy day at the clinic, and Mack realized that this was the first seat she'd had since before lunchtime. She leaned over and nudged her arm against Jessica's. "So how're things?"

Jessica glanced up and then returned her attention to her feet. "Good."

Mack sucked air through her teeth and regarded the girl through narrowed eyes. "Lewis was telling me that some things have been said in class."

Jessica glanced up.

"Now don't be mad at him. He's just worried 'bout you."

Closing her eyes Jessica gulped. "They said that my family isn't normal. That I'm not normal," she said quietly.

Letting out a 'humph,' Mack looked up at the darkening sky. "Hell Jessica, no family is normal when you scratch the surface, especially the families in Grace Falls. It's like this town is a breeding ground for the weird and wonderful." She dropped her gaze to look at Jessica. "And I include my family in there," she added with a soft nudge. "But let me tell you something about your family," she said, taking Jessica's hands and resting them both in her lap. "Your parents love you so much, and they wanted you so badly that they had to overcome obstacles to get you. Big boulders that most folks don't have to come across. Do you know how lucky you are? I'd say fifty percent of your class are on this earth because of one too many at the Sports Bar. In fact, a number of them are here just 'cause their parent's team won the Iron Bowl that year." She stopped and looked wistfully into the middle distance. "Good times," she muttered under her breath, recalling the circumstances of an Auburn victory that lead to her own pregnancy. She shook her head to get back on track. "Your parents love you, and that's the most important fact in your life."

Jessica leaned into Mack and rested her head against the nurse's arm. "They said stuff about my mama and Maddie too," she said, gripping Mack's hand tighter.

"Sweetie, you've always known that your mama liked women. She's never hidden that from you," Mack said softly.

Twisting her head so she could look into Mack's eyes Jessica shrugged. "My mama says I'm smart for my age and I know stuff, but she also says that knowing and understanding are different, and the understanding bit can take longer."

Mack smiled. When she spoke to Jessica, she was always surprised by her insight and intelligence. Both were far beyond her years. The nurse suspected that her preference for the company of adults over children while she was growing up, and her ability to hold her own in conversation, was a result of being the firstborn into the tight-knit group of friends. The adults in her life always treated her like a small adult; never babying her and always telling her the truth.

It made Mack despair slightly when she compared Jessica to Lewis, who was only a couple of months younger than Jessica. Indeed had Jessica not been so eager to start her life early, he would have been older than her. Only one week before, Mack had returned home from work to be greeted with the joy of extracting yet another Lego piece from her son's nasal cavity. What he was trying to do by continually thrusting the plastic pieces up there was beyond Mack.

The nurse's mouth quirked into a small smirk when she thought about her son. What he may lack in common sense and self-control when it came to Danish-made construction toys, he more than compensated for with the size of his heart; a heart that from the first day in kindergarten had boundless love for Jessica. It had been his return home from school the previous day with an arm full of scratches that had alerted Mack to the comments being made. Eventually, and after much prompting, the young boy had admitted that they had come as a result of his attempts to stop the guilty culprits from repeating their jibes.

"You're right," Mack said. "Always knowing your mama is gay is different from understanding what that means. Do you like Maddie?"

Jessica's face creased into the familiar Milne smile.

"I'll take that as a yes." Mack smiled in return. "What it means is that your mama deserves to be loved by someone like Maddie and whatever anyone says to you, you remember that. She deserves to love and be loved just like everyone on this planet." She put her arm around Jessica and pulled her close. "There is not one wrong thing about love. Hate, through ignorance and intolerance. That is wrong. But love; love is never wrong and don't let anyone tell you otherwise."

Jessica nodded thoughtfully as she weighed up Mack's words. "I love you, Mack," she said, snuggling closer into her hug.

Mack chuckled and squeezed Jessica against her. "Good, 'cause I'm planning on being your mama-in-law. So just you remember you said that when I'm criticizing your Thanksgiving dinner."

The two fell into a companionable silence until the door opened behind them and Maddie appeared with Emmett Day.

∞ ∞ ∞

The two cups of iced tea wobbled precariously as Jessica waved enthusiastically through the glass door of Sullivan's Sports Bar. Her father's broad smile was visible through the shaded bar as he waved in return and walked towards the door to unlock it. He pulled the door open and reached for one of the cups. "One of those for me?"

"Nuh-uh," Jessica replied, smacking his hand away. "I'm going to the clinic."

"I figured," Sully replied, jokingly rubbing the back of his hand. "You coming over for dinner tonight? Lou's made pecan pie, and she can't eat it so I could use some help."

Jessica twisted her mouth considering the offer. "Can I use the computer?"

"Nope." Sully grinned and planted a kiss on her forehead.

"You're ruining my education," Jessica grumbled, as her father slipped back through the door.

"We're keeping you out of jail," Sully countered from behind the glass door. He waved his fingers dismissing his daughter. "See you at six thirty, or there will be no pie left."

Jessica's lips curled into a snarl. "Do something once," she muttered, as she turned to continue her journey to the clinic.

She pulled open the fly-screen and entered the clinic building. The breeze from the ceiling fan was doing nothing to take the edge off the stifling heat. She was glad that, following a period of fundraising by the town the defunct air conditioning, which the fans were admirably but ultimately failing to replace, was due to be removed and upgraded. This had been the cause of much celebration in their home. Maddie had ritually moaned her way through the previous two summers.

"Please tell me they're what I think they are," Mack asked, looking over the top of the reception desk.

Jessica grinned. "Iced teas courtesy of Ruby's." She placed the tray on the desk and frowned at the small boy sitting swiveling on the office chair. "Is everything okay with Aunt Ruth?" she asked nodding toward Ben who was smiling broadly at Jessica as he spun around.

Mack took a long sip of the drink, letting out a satisfied moan. "She's fine, it's time," she said. "We're just waiting on the babysitter coming to take Ben here home." Mack reached over and stopped the spinning chair that had picked up an impressive momentum and ruffled the boy's dark curls.

"Mack!" Maddie's head popped around one of the exam room doors. "Oh, hey, squirt." She grinned at spotting Jessica.

"Hey, Maddie," Jessica replied. "I'll look after Ben if you need to go," she said to Mack. The nurse mouthed a thank you and squeezed Jessica's shoulders as she passed by. "Hey, Ben." Jessica smiled, entering the area behind the desk. "You're going to be a big brother soon." Ben nodded, and his eyes widened as he looked at the older girl. "You realize that being a big brother is a big responsibility," Jessica continued as she lifted Ben from the chair and slipped beneath the three-year-old. She plopped him onto her lap as she began to repeat the words that had been said to her recently. "Your little brother or sister will look up to you. You have to help show them what's right and what's wrong and computer hacking is always very wrong." She chuckled to herself while remembering her mother's serious face during their chat. "You have to have their back. Even though sometimes you want to kick them, they're yours, and you have to protect what's yours."

Their heads lifted as they heard Ruth yell from the exam room.

"Okay, I'm fairly certain that's a don't repeat word," Jessica whispered tightening her grip on Ben as he squirmed to get out of her grip.

"Mama hurt," he said, pointing towards the room.

"Nooo, Mama's not hurt"—Jessica said—"she's just excited that your brother or sister is coming."

"'cited?" Ben looked at her questioningly.

"Yup just excited"—Jessica replied emphatically—"and anyway if she was hurt my mom's in there with her and she's awesome."

Maddie stood around the corner from the reception desk. Her hand clutched her chest. She'd come out to grab some ice cubes for Ruth when she'd heard Jessica's voice repeating Alex's words. She had been standing silently listening, and proud of Jessica as she spoke to Ben when for the first time she heard Jessica refer to her as her mother. She choked back the lump in her throat and gave a businesslike nod before making her presence known. "Okay, I heard there's an iced tea out here with my name on it," she said brightly, striding around the desk to pick her cup up.

"Is everything okay?" Jessica asked.

"Everything is going to plan." Maddie smiled before her expression wavered as the door to the clinic burst open behind her and she spun around to see who had entered.

"It's happening." Sully's excited voice boomed through the clinic. "Maddie, it's happening!"

Maddie put her cup down. "Well, where is she?" she asked, leaning to look past Sully. Waddling up the pathway to the clinic was a heavily pregnant Lou, her hands clasped under her bump as if holding it up. "Sully!" Maddie yelled, slapping the man out of the way and stepping out to help Lou up the stairs to the clinic.

Jessica watched as Maddie guided Lou into an exam room. Her father practically tripped over his feet as he followed. He disappeared around the corner then reappeared a second later with a broad grin on his face. "It's happening," he repeated, as he leaned over and kissed his daughter's head, before disappearing again.

"Looks like we're both going to have a brother or sister today," she remarked to the boy sitting on her lap, before using her feet to spin them both around.

∞ ∞ ∞

Two hours later and Ben was at home with the babysitter, unaware that he now had a little sister. Jessica, however, was still waiting to find out what sex her sibling would be. She had moved from the reception desk and was now lounging in the waiting room where she was joined periodically by a combination of Peter, Mack, her father or Maddie. She had started to pace back and forth counting the number of steps between the edge of the waiting room and the reception desk. It had been twenty on the first count and twenty-two on the second. Her third recount was interrupted when the front door opened. She looked up, and her eyes widened. "Maddie. Mack," she yelled.

Mack stuck her head out of the exam room where she was with Lou. "What the hell you yelling for?" She stopped and allowed her mouth to drop. "You have got to be kidding me." She shook her head at the sight of Douglas supporting a panting Teddy who had one hand protectively covering her large bump. Mack turned her face back into the room. "Doc, we got another one. Teddy and Douglas have decided to join the party."

Jessica heard Maddie's cursed response to the news. "Exam room three's free." Jessica smiled. "Why don't I take you there?" She led the nervous expectant father and still panting Teddy towards the room, earning a wink from Mack before the nurse ducked back into the room to relieve Maddie.

One hour later Jessica had a little sister. She was taken into the room and allowed to hold her; as long as she sat still. When her dad placed the tiny baby in her arms, she gently kissed her new sister's soft forehead. "I will teach you all the fun stuff, I promise," she whispered.

Maddie watched Jessica interact with her new sister and felt the lump that she had swallowed earlier reappear. She felt Sully's arm circle her shoulder as the proud dad watched his two daughters acquaint themselves.

"Maddie." Mack popped her head around the door. "Teddy's close now and you probably want to get out here."

Maddie nodded and gave Sully's puffed out chest a pat. "You did good, Daddy." She smiled over towards a weary-looking Lou, whose head was tipped to the side, her eyes never leaving her daughter. "You did better, Mommy." She grinned then slipped out of the door. The passageway between the examination rooms was empty, save for a panicked-looking Sam.

"Hey, Sam." Maddie greeted him. "Everything okay?"

Sam nodded wildly.

"Room four." He pointed.

Maddie frowned and looked at the room then back to Sam who was still pointing. She walked slowly towards the room wondering what had Sam looking so worried, as she pushed the door open the reason for his expression was apparent.

"Oh. My. God." Maddie exclaimed. Bending over and clutching onto the bed rail with one hand, with the other wrapped around her swollen belly, was Alex. Her face was contorted, and sweat was beading on her forehead.

"I tried to hold off coming. I heard the others were in labor, so I tried." Alex started to apologize.

"Were you planning on crossing your legs and hoping our baby just didn't appear?" Maddie replied, rushing to her side. "Besides, if they're all born today Sully owes me a thousand bucks." She grinned as she helped Alex onto the bed.

"What's the count so far?" Alex asked through gritted teeth, as another contraction started to tear through her.

"Two girls," Maddie answered quickly. Her mind was focused on getting Alex settled so she could examine her. "Teddy's just about to pop. That's what all the yelling and swearing is about," she said, referring to the ever-increasing array of expletives coming from down the hall.

"Do you need to go?" Alex gasped, as she fought the urge to push.

Smiling, Maddie placed a kiss on Alex's lips. "Nope. I'm right where I need to be."

"Actually, I think you need to be somewhere else." Alex groaned and nodded between her legs. Maddie raised an eyebrow and was about to make a smart remark when Alex's expression halted her. "I think your son is about to appear and it would be really good if you caught him," she practically roared.

Maddie chuckled at Alex's comment. She slipped Alex's maternity trousers and underwear off and gasped as she spotted the baby's head. "You weren't joking! How long were you putting off coming in?" She looked wide-eyed at Alex who was biting her bottom lip and concentrating on trying to breathe through the contractions. "Well alright," Maddie said. "C'mon little one. You have two mommies who can't wait to see your face."

Five minutes later Teddy gave birth to a boy.

A minute later Alan Milne-Marinelli was born.

∞ ∞ ∞

Alex watched through exhausted and tear-filled eyes as Maddie put their son into a grinning Jessica's arms. "Hey, little bear." Jessica smiled, ignoring the sounds of stifled sobs coming from Alex and sniffing from Maddie. "I'm your big sister, and these two crying wrecks are our moms. Welcome to our family."

Epilogue

Part Two

Maddie pushed the door handle down and entered the room. She narrowed her eyes as she tried to pick out a clear path towards the bed in the darkness. She peeked over Alan's shoulder as she edged slowly towards the prone figure in the bed. She reached out and flipped on the lamp. She couldn't help but give a small smile as Jessica's face scrunched up in complaint at the light's intrusion on her sleep. The doctor bent her knees to reach down. She moved carefully to not disturb the dozing toddler in her arms and removed the heavy open textbook resting on Jessica's chest. She rolled her eyes as she lifted the book and inspected the title. "Cardiology! Honestly, Zoe, corrupting young innocent minds." She huffed to herself and placed the book carefully on the nightstand. "Squirt, time to get up." Jessica made an unintelligible noise and turned away from the light. "Jessica, count of three then I get the water jug," Maddie said firmly.

"Mooooomm," groaned Jessica as she twisted her head and popped one eye open. "Do we have to do this?"

Maddie still got a kick out of hearing Jessica call her Mom. Since Alan's birth, the girl had started to use the term directly when speaking to her more and more. "Your mama's already gone to help your dad set up, and everyone's going to be there. So, yes, we have to do this."

"It's the middle of the night." Jessica moaned as she pulled herself into a sitting position. "What are you wearing?!" She looked in horror at Maddie's outfit.

Maddie looked down and held the hem of her T-shirt out. "We're all wearing them." She shifted the still-dozing Alan in her arms to show Jessica his T-shirt. The small boy huffed and wound his chubby arms tighter around his mother's neck, releasing hold of the soft toy that accompanied his every move.

Jessica shook her head as she spun her legs out of her bed and crouched down to retrieve the stuffed toy skunk. "No way. I'm not wearing one."

"Um, yes you are," Maddie replied, shifting her position so she could toss Jessica's T-shirt down onto the bed. "Your mama made these. If I'm wearing it, you're wearing it." She took the skunk from Jessica's outstretched hand and turned to leave the room. "We'll see you downstairs in twenty, squirt."

"So uncool." Jessica flopped back onto her bed and lay looking at the ceiling.

∞ ∞ ∞

Maddie opened the door to Sullivan's Sports Bar. Each time she entered the bar her eyes were drawn to the altered sign on the door. She was almost disappointed that Sully had given up replacing it. The group of friends would often watch with amusement as the bar owner would be left scratching his head and muttering about a 'wise-ass' after the sign was changed back to Sullivan's Sports Bra practically overnight. In all the years that it had been happening, Sully still had no idea that the wise-ass was Alex.

She held the door open while Jessica entered carrying Alan on her hip. Sully looked up from behind the counter and smiled. "We've set up a sleep zone in the office for the rug rats, and we're planning on putting Ruth in there when she gets cranky." He grinned and nodded his head towards the door before he ducked a towel that was thrown in his direction by Ruth.

Jessica and Maddie opened the door to the office quietly so as not to disturb those inside. An inflatable mattress dominated the floor space and in the middle was a softly snoring Ben flanked by his sister and cousin. Jessica lowered Alan onto the mattress and covered him over. Satisfied that he was going to remain asleep, they backed their way out of the office and headed back to the bar.

"So what can we do to help?" Maddie asked rolling the sleeves of her sweatshirt up.

"You managed to just arrive as we're done." Alex smiled, swatting Maddie's butt. "Everyone should be arriving any minute." She kissed Maddie on the lips. "I hope you're wearing your T-shirt under that sweatshirt."

Maddie tugged on Alex's T-shirt stopping her from moving away. "I'm more interested in what's under your T-shirt." She smirked.

Alex felt the heat rise in her cheeks. "Much more of that and we'll be kicking the kids off that mattress, and giving this a miss."

Jessica brushed past carrying a pile of flags. "No way you two are disappearing off. If I'm here in the middle of the night wearing a stupid T-shirt you're both staying."

The two women rolled their eyes and separated.

Alex skipped after Jessica and grabbed her daughter around the waist. "You're such a little grump when you're tired." She nuzzled her face into Jessica's neck as the teenager started to giggle.

"Mama, I'll drop the flags." Jessica laughed, dropping her head to the side to rest it against her mother's.

"Can't have you doing that," Alex replied, planting a loud kiss on Jessica's cheek.

The door to the bar opened, and Douglas and Teddy arrived. Teddy held out a platter full of food. "Where do you want this?" she called, shrugging her jacket off. "I wasn't sure what kind of food you make for the middle of the night."

"Doesn't matter what it is." Maddie shrugged lifting a sausage from the platter and popping it in her mouth. "Food never tastes the same during the night. Don't get Mack started on the subject or we'll miss the race."

Alex took the platter from her and smiled at Douglas, who was carrying his sleeping son in his right arm and a car seat holding a babbling baby girl in his left. "I'll take this and put it with the rest, and you can pop Sleepy there in the office with the other little humans." She looked down at Teddy and Douglas' daughter. "And you, big girl, can help your Aunt Madeleine stop eating all the food." She looked pointedly at Maddie whose hand was in midair towards the platter.

"Right." Maddie grinned. "I'll take you." She took the car seat from Douglas and lifted it up whispering to the baby as she walked further into the bar. "We'll just go this way and see what other food there is."

Half an hour later and the bar was filled with more Grace Falls residents than Maddie had seen in a long time in one place. Had it not been for the clock telling her it was two in the morning she would have thought it was a Friday evening with the bustle and energy the bar exuded. As the big screen flickered into life, the occupants of the bar turned their attention towards the end of the bar, eager to watch perhaps the biggest event that Grace Falls had ever seen.

The noise started to increase as the commentator mentioned the name that they were all there to support.

"Sweatshirts off you two." Alex nudged Maddie and her daughter who both reluctantly removed their tops to reveal their 'Team Hunter' shirts.

Sam took his position on the start line. He was clad in the dark blue lycra of Team USA. Sully shushed everyone and turned the sound up on the commentary.

"It's a lovely afternoon here in Pyeongchang, and the competitors are lining up for the mass start Biathlon. Sam Hunter, our home interest in this one, has the most intriguing story. Sam hails from a small town back in Alabama called Grace Falls, where I'm told they don't actually get a great deal of snow, so it should be interesting to see how he copes here."

Mack leaped from her chair, her clenched fist punching the air above her. "You give 'em hell, Sam."

Maddie laughed at her nurse's outburst. "She's been excited all week." She murmured against Alex's hair. Alex leaned back against the warmth of Maddie's body.

"Yeah, but did she make T-shirts?!" Alex replied, never taking her eyes off the screen.

Maddie grinned and let her eyes wander around the bar. Sully was standing behind the bar leaning over the counter to kiss Lou, as she bounced their daughter up and down. Peter, Ruth, Teddy, and Douglas were sitting at the table that they habitually sat at on a Friday evening. Their children, now wide awake thanks to the noise from the bar, were shared out amongst them. Jessica was now down at the front of the bar near the big screen with Lewis. Sitting on her lap watching with wide eyes was Alan with his toy skunk firmly in his grasp. Maddie twisted her head towards the bar and smiled as she spotted the photographs in pride of place on the wall. The first was a graduation photo. The younger versions of the faces that Maddie had just scanned looked back out at her along with the face that she had never seen in real life. Next to it was a photo of Sully and Alex during Jessica's sign ceremony. The largest photo was of the friends with all of their children taken during what was billed as the biggest sign ceremony the town had ever hosted. She took in a deep breath, and a satisfied smile appeared on her lips.

"You okay?" Alex asked, tipping her head back so she could see Maddie.

"I'm wonderful."

"So why the big sigh?"

Maddie pulled Alex closer to her and rested her chin on her shoulder. "I was just counting my blessings and thanking God for car trouble."

About the Author

H.P. Munro lives in London with her wife and a wauzer named Boo. She started writing in 2010 when a new job took her away from home a lot and she found herself in airports, on flights and in hotel rooms with room service for one. The job didn't last but the love of writing did.

Her début novel Silver Wings won the Golden Crown Literary Society Historical Fiction award in 2014. Her novels Grace Falls and Stars Collide were published in 2014 and quickly became lesbian romance bestsellers with Stars Collide selected as a finalist in the Goldies 2015 Traditional Contemporary Romance category.

You can connect with HP through:
Email: munrohp@gmail.com
Facebook: www.facebook.com/munrohp
Twitter: @munrohp
Website: www.red-besom-books.com

Other Titles by Author

SAVING GRACE

ISBN-13: 978-1537319117
ASIN: B01M9BKTI4

When Charlotte Grace left Grace Falls at the age of seventeen, she swore she'd never return. More than twenty years on she still regrets breaking the heart of her first love. Reaching a crossroads in her life, Charlotte has started to merely drift along.

Erin Hunter has spent a lifetime recovering from having her heart shattered by the person she trusted most. Taking shelter in her home town and her career, she's avoided relationships.

Neither woman ever thought they'd see each other again. They didn't count on Grace Falls. The quirky town's charm pulls people in, and if the town isn't enough, its residents are more than willing to lend a hand.

Celebrate a return to Grace Falls.

SILVER WINGS

WINNER - 2014 Golden Crown Literary Society – Historical Fiction

ISBN-13: 978-1482023572

ASIN: B00FXY3LTU

When in 1942, twenty-five-year-old Lily Rivera is widowed, she finally feels able to step out of the shadows of an unhappy marriage. Her love of flying leads her to join the Womens Airforce Service Pilots, determined to regain her passion and spread her wings, no suspecting that she would experience more than just flying.

Helen Richmond, a Hollywood stunt pilot, has never experienced a love that lifted her as high as the aircraft she flew...until she meets Lily. Both women join the W.A.S.P. program to serve their country and instead find that they are on a collision course towards each other, but can it last?

STARS COLLIDE

FINALIST – 2015 Golden Crown Literary Society – Traditional Contemporary Romance

Amazon Best Seller - #1 Lesbian Romance, #1 Lesbian Fiction

ISBN-13: 978-1499357776
ASIN: B00KHAEHTI

It's tough growing up in the spotlight and Freya Easter has had to do just that, being part of the Conor family, who are Hollywood acting royalty, has meant that every aspect of her family's life has been played out in the spotlight. Despite her own fame Freya has managed to keep one aspect of her life out of the public eye, however, a new job on hit show Front Line and a storyline that pairs her with the gorgeous Jordan Ellis, may mean that Freya's secret is about to come out.

In a world of glitz and glamor, Jordan Ellis has come to the conclusion that all that glitters is not gold. She has become disillusioned with relationships and is longing for a deeper connection, and is surprised when it comes in the form of the most unexpected package.

Made in the USA
Columbia, SC
21 July 2019